FROZEN HEIGHTS

A DEEPWOOD MOUNTAIN COMPLETE SERIES

LEXI HAYES

Published by No Regerts Press, LLC

NO REGERTS
PRESS, LLC

Cover Designed by Cormar Covers

ISBN 978-1-957933-40-5 (print)

Join my mailing list here:
www.lexihayes.com

CONTENTS

CLAIMED BY THE BURLY EX-CON

TRAPPED WITH THE GROWLY ROCK STAR

CAPTURED BY THE BRAWNY VETERAN

RESCUED BY THE RUGGED PRINCE

CLAIMED BY THE BURLY EX-CON

CHAPTER 1
PENNY

"You're officially crazy," JJ says, placing the stack of comic books on my desk.

I grab a couple of the comics in their plastic protective sleeves and lean back in my chair, putting my feet up while being careful to avoid my bobblehead Marvel figurines.

"Why? Because I want to deliver these in person? I've done it before." I thumb through the rare DC titles. They're editions from the '70s that I haven't seen before. I'm not a huge fan of the DC universe myself, but I can admire anyone who has this kind of dedication to seek out the older stuff.

"Yes, Penny, but not to strangers." JJ and I both started as volunteers for the Deepwood Mountain Library when we were in high school. JJ went full-time after she graduated and became a library assistant. I got a degree in IT and was able to come back here and snag a job as a support technician. I mostly work with our e-systems but have also spearheaded some programming for our emerging fandom hub.

"And especially not strangers up in Frozen Heights," she adds.

"So?"

"*So* it's way up in the mountains, a total storm magnet, and a lot of the residents there are…you know… kinda rough around the edges." She perches on the corner of my desk and fiddles with the buttons on her cardigan. JJ reminds me of a modern-day Snow White, if Snow White had pink streaks in her shiny black hair. Super innocent, and a little protective of me besides. But as my roommate and best friend, I guess she's allowed.

We've all heard the stories about Frozen Heights. How it's filled with shady individuals looking to disappear for…whatever reason.

But who am I to judge?

"Where's your sense of adventure?" I laugh, glancing up at my *Avengers* poster.

She huffs and crosses her arms over her chest.

"Come on, JJ—I bet most people up there are just looking for some peace and quiet. I wouldn't believe all the rumors." Large, fluffy snowflakes float to the ground outside our office window. "And I mean, yeah, it's snowing, but not nearly enough to make a fuss about." I wave off her worries dismissively.

"That's because it's still early," she frets. "The *real* storm won't hit until later this evening, and it's supposed to be a doozy! I'm sure Deepwood will be completely covered, and it will be even worse up there. You think you can just bounce into Frozen Heights and back again?" She shakes her head. "It's not just the weather, either: there are no streetlights up there, and the roads are narrow and icy. You'll be putting yourself in real danger."

I swing my feet off the desk and lean forward. "JJ, you know me. I'm always safer than safe. Since the mail's already been collected, these won't get to Mr. Brooks until late Monday at the earliest. If a storm's coming, wouldn't it be awesome for him to be able to enjoy these over a snowed-in weekend?"

She rolls her hazel eyes. "He won't need the comics for entertainment if he has you tied up in the basement."

"JJ!" I sputter. "And you say *I* have a wild imagination?"

"Well... No one can say you don't go above and beyond for our readers."

I flash her a smile and stand up, removing my favorite blue and green flannel from around my waist. I pull it over my Captain Marvel T-shirt before grabbing my coat and beanie from the rack nearby. Paired with my trusty fleece-lined black jeans and combat boots, I'm ready. Mrs. Holloway retired a few months ago, and we sure do miss her, but oh man, the dress code is *much* more chill now. Insert happy dance here.

"I really can't change your mind?" she asks.

"Nope. The snow isn't that bad, and I'm sure Mr. Brooks is just a harmless comic book enthusiast."

"Or a total weirdo."

I lick my lips. "In that case, he and I will get along fine. It's normal people I have trouble with."

"Hey! You get along great with me."

I shrug. "You said it, not me."

She throws up her hands. "You're impossible."

I laugh and give her a hug. "I know how to handle comic book geeks, okay?"

JJ sighs, knowing she's lost the battle. "Fine, but be careful, please. Keep checking in, and for god's sake, if anything seems off, *turn back*. I'm serious, Penny."

"I will, I promise," I say, booping her on the nose.

After I've filled my thermos with hot coffee, I'm on my way in my little truck. The snow has indeed picked up, the swirling snowflakes creating a beautiful but disorienting pattern before my windshield. As I drive along the winding mountain road, I force myself to focus, keeping my eyes peeled for the turnoff for Frozen Heights.

When I finally spot it, the way forward looks serene, almost ethereal. But then the road gradually narrows and the snow deepens, and no matter how slowly and carefully I go, my truck slips and slides with each twist and turn.

Eventually, I start to see mailboxes at the edges of tiny driveways. I spot Mr. Brooks' number and turn up the incline, and a cabin with smoke puffing cheerfully from the chimney comes into view.

I park as close to the front door as possible. The snow is still falling heavily, the tops of large bushes the only markers showing me the path through. I carefully tuck the comics into my coat and zip it up tight before heading out.

Shoot. It's colder than I expected it would be. Each step is a challenge, my boots sinking into the knee-deep—sometimes deeper—snow. The wind whips around me, and I'm thankful for my warm knitted hat. I have to squint against the stinging snowflakes, and the wind is face-hurting cold, but I press on.

Just as I'm making good progress, I take a step that has me falling further than I anticipate.

Snow collapses in quickly over my head.

Shit.

I yell for help, but the snow muffles my words, and I'm sure no one could hear me over the wind anyway. I struggle to free myself, but I only bring in more snow and darkness around me, sinking even deeper.

Oh god...I'm going to suffocate!

Sheer panic has me scrambling to dig myself out, but my limbs are rapidly getting colder and I can barely move with how packed in the snow is around me. If I don't suffocate, the very real threat of freezing to death suddenly seems a terrifying possibility.

I'm going to die, right here in Mr. Brooks' front yard.

They won't find me till spring, like that guy in *The Shining*.

Wish I had superpowers now...

Suddenly, something—some*one*—pulls me out of the snow-bank, effortlessly lifting me up. I take a big gasping breath once I'm out in the cold air, my heart pounding as relief slams through my body.

CHAPTER 2
MITCH

As the snowstorm rages outside, its icy claws tearing at the cabin walls, I'm thankful I chopped enough wood to last me the weekend. If I'm snowed in, at least I'll be warm.

I got lucky finding this place. A buddy of mine mentioned Frozen Heights as a good place to get back on track, now that I've done my time and am out of prison for good. Peaceful and quiet, you know? And the cabin itself is modest, clean, and cozy, with everything I need to start over and figure out the next steps in my life.

I sit back in the recliner, watching the snow outside come down hard and fast. My mug of freshly brewed tea warms my hands as I take a sip, letting the steam fog up my reading glasses.

Then I spot it in my peripheral vision—a pop of color through the blanket of white outside.

I swear it's a woman, with long chestnut hair.

Ripping off my glasses, I jump up toward the window.

Shit.

She's gone. Completely swallowed up by the snowbank.

I instinctively spring into action, shrugging on my thick jacket and pulling on a woolen hat. In moments, I'm out the door and wading through the deep snow, digging away at it with my arms.

After a few sweeping movements, I see the fuzzy ball at the top of a hat. She must be buried below.

I reach down, my hands feeling around to get a good hold and then pulling her from the icy prison. Her body is petite and soft, wrapped in a puffy coat and jeans.

She gasps for air.

"Breathe, baby," I hear myself say. Strange. Why would I call this woman such a thing? She's a stranger.

"I'm t-try-ing to…" she whispers, teeth chattering.

I haul her into my arms and she looks up at me, her deep blue-gray eyes wide, like a startled doe. Her cheeks are pink from the cold, with a smattering of freckles. She looks young. Definitely too young for me to be staring at her pretty pale lips as they part in surprise.

"M-Mr. Brooks?" she stutters.

The sound of my name spoken by her voice, trembling from the cold, tugs at something low and deep within me. Without hesitation, I gather her closer, cradling her against my chest as I head back to the front door.

"It's okay, I've got you," I reassure her. "Let's get you inside."

I stomp the snow from my boots and make my way to the couch in front of the fireplace, letting her body sink into the cushions. Kneeling in front of her, I remove her gloves and take her hands in mine, rubbing them gently to warm them. My large hands dwarf her tiny ones.

"Here," I say, reaching for a thick, warm blanket. "Let me help you out of your coat. You're still shivering."

She just nods, watching me unzip her jacket. A few plastic-covered—magazines, maybe?—fall out and she carefully slides them to the side. Once her coat is off, I wrap the blanket around her shoulders.

Her eyes dart around my cabin. "I'm Penny," she says, giving me a small smile that has my cock already at attention. "Penny Evanson."

"Penny, huh? That's an adorable name." My eyes travel over her sweet face, landing again briefly on her lush lips. God, I need to get it together or this girl is gonna run away screaming.

"Mitch Brooks. But please, just call me Mitch." I tuck the blanket more closely around her, wanting any excuse to touch her. "Wasn't expecting company tonight. Especially not in this weather."

She licks her lips and I stifle a groan, unable to look away. "I'm from the Deepwood Library. I—I came to deliver the comic books you requested."

Right, I remember now: I placed a hold on some special edition DC titles.

"I appreciate you coming all the way out here, but you didn't need to. I thought I asked for them to be mailed."

Penny grins. "I wanted to get them to you for the weekend. Thought I could beat the storm. Comics are kinda my thing, and I wanted to make a fellow fan happy, even though I'll admit I'm more Team Marvel than DC."

I chuckle. "That's sweet," I say, patting her knee before getting up and hanging our coats and hats on the rack near the door. "Let me get you something hot to drink. You must be frozen to the bone."

"Oh, you don't have to go to any trouble. I'll just warm myself by the fire."

"Nonsense," I say from the kitchen. "We almost lost you to the elements when you were delivering my comic books. The least I can do is pour you some tea. I've already made a whole pot."

She chuckles. "Ironic, right? Almost dying delivering books about superheroes."

I laugh and return with a steaming mug.

"Anyway, you're definitely my hero," she says, her eyes brighter now. She wraps her hands around the cup and takes an appreciative sip. "I thought I'd never feel my fingers again."

"You should take off your boots and get your feet warm, too." I glance out the window at the snow piling up quickly. "It's not safe out there, and it probably won't be for a while."

She follows my gaze out the window. "JJ's going to kill me."

My heart sinks. Of course she has a boyfriend. Maybe even husband.

"JJ?" I ask as casually as I can.

"She works with me at the library. She also happens to be my roommate. She told me not to come." She laughs. "Said only shady types live up here, too."

She's not *totally* wrong. "She's smart."

"Hey!" Penny says, tossing one of her wet socks my way. "What does that say about me?"

I laugh and lay the sock out in front of the fire to dry. "I didn't mean it like that. It's just not everyday someone delivers comic books straight to my door." I pause. "Or *almost* to my door."

She laughs and stretches her bare feet toward the fire. "Thank you again. I'm glad you happened to see me when you did. Not sure I would've made it if you hadn't."

Probably not. The thought sends a shuddering surge of

protectiveness through me. Like it's my duty to keep her safe from now on.

"You should probably text JJ to let her know where you are. I'd be worried sick if I was her."

"Ooh, you're right." She pulls her phone from her pocket, and I watch as her fingers deftly send a quick message.

Her thumbs fly over the screen, and I can tell she's texting back and forth. Finally, she puts it away. "She's still worried. But I told her I didn't think there's a basement in this place for you to tie me up in."

I spit out my tea. "I'm sorry? You did *not* just tell her that."

A grin spreads over her face, and she laughs.

"You're trouble, Penny Evanson," I say with a chuckle, shaking my head and running a hand through my hair. This woman's a pistol, that's for sure.

She bites her lip, studying me a little too hard. I like her eyes on me. But I can't help but worry if she thinks I look a bit rough, what with all the tattoos and the scruffy beard. Do I *look* like an ex-con? I haven't spent much time out in the world since my release, and I'm honestly not sure how people see me now. Can they tell where I've spent the last three years of my life?

I turn toward the kitchen. "Can I make us some dinner? I have a couple of thawed steaks and some potatoes I can mash."

"Sounds wonderful, thank you," she says, looking over the back of the couch. "I can help, too. I'm a decent cook."

"I'm sure you are, but tonight, you're my guest." I turn on the stove. "You can keep me company while I cook, though. Why don't you tell me what got you into comic books? Most women your age seem to prefer what...*Twilight*? Or those monster romance novels?"

She rolls her eyes as she takes a sip of her tea. "Oh my god,

Mitch. Way to stereotype." She pauses for a moment. "*Twilight* has its moments…and monster romance *is* pretty hot."

I look up from seasoning the steaks and arch a skeptical brow.

She laughs. "But as for comics…I fell in love with the Marvel universe when I was a kid. My dad's a fan, and he handed his collection down to me. It was our special daddy-daughter bonding time—reading and talking about them, watching the movies together. I still go to him sometimes if there's a burning superhero or plot question on my mind."

I nod. "Sounds like your dad's a cool guy. It's awesome how comics can bring people together. That's what I love about them, too—the stories, the art. They're like an escape and a connection to something greater." I drop the meat into an iron skillet, and it sizzles loudly.

When I turn back to her, she's staring at me open-mouthed. "What?" I pat myself down like maybe I forgot to button my shirt, or that my fly is unzipped. Then I remember I'm wearing sweatpants and a sweatshirt.

"I'm just…impressed." She looks up at me in—is that awe? —and I get a *great* view of her Captain Marvel T-shirt, not to mention the way her large breasts stretch the fabric. I tamp down my arousal as she continues. "I'm leading a program at the library for fandoms of all kinds. You should check it out sometime."

"Now it's my turn to be impressed," I say, grabbing the potatoes from the pantry. "That sounds right up my alley. You're full of surprises, Penny. Though I'm afraid your taste in comic universes leaves something to be desired."

"Oh, we are *not* going to go there, mister."

I laugh. "Why not?"

She hops up to sit on the kitchen counter, possibly trying to look taller as an intimidation technique. I know that game.

But I've never gotten to play it with a sexy woman like Penny.

"Marvel's universe is far more realistic, more relatable, and just…grittier all around," she states.

"*And* more violent," I add.

She opens her mouth to speak, then closes it again and tilts her head, thinking. Guess she hadn't expected that. "Okay, I'll give you that."

"And…I'm sorry, grittier? What's grittier than Gotham?" I continue.

"Almost everywhere a Marvel character exists…on Earth, *or elsewhere.*"

"Hmm… Is that all you got?" I tease, letting the potatoes come to a boil, then flipping the steaks.

She crosses her arms over her magnificent chest and lifts her chin. "Marvel superheroes are all around more powerful."

I grab a couple of plates from the cupboard. "But DC has heroes that don't even *have* superpowers. They're just regular humans that happen to be exceptional. Like Batman. He has to rely on his intellect and training."

"And silly gadgets."

"I can't believe you just called Batman's gear silly."

"He's a billionaire with a god complex."

I choke and start coughing.

She grabs my forearm. "Oh my god, are you okay?" My skin electrifies under her fingers.

I nod. "It's just the…audacity," I finally manage to get out, and she laughs musically, the sound like the tinkling of windchimes.

She looks down at where she's touching me. "Wait. Is that…?" She pulls my wrist closer to her face and then grins at me. "A *Superman* tattoo?"

I chuckle, liking that she feels comfortable enough to touch me…even if she is teasing me about my tattoos. Grr.

She's so close. I could lean down and kiss her right now, punishing that blasphemous mouth for saying such disparaging things about Batman.

But the steaks would burn.

"It is. One of the many DC tats I have." I very reluctantly pull out of her grip to plate the steaks.

She whistles and shakes her head. "You really are dedicated."

I notice some ink on her wrist. "Hey now, I see a tattoo there. How many Marvel tattoos do *you* have, Missy?" I tease, letting the meat rest while I drain the potatoes.

She mumbles something under her breath.

"I'm sorry, say that again?" I grin.

"Five," she says more clearly, her smile sheepish.

"Nice. Maybe you'll show me sometime." I start mashing the potatoes.

"I'll show you mine if you show me yours."

My grip on the masher slips for a moment, and Penny's face turns a delightful shade of crimson. "I'm sorry, that was… I'm so bad at this."

"Bad at what?"

"Nothing," she hedges, worrying that sweet lower lip. "Just…you are…"

"Intimidating?" I finish, adding some cream and butter to the potatoes, then going back to pounding them with the masher. Yeah, I must be scary to a five-foot-nothing angel.

She nods, looking down at the counter. "Maybe, a little. But it's not that. You're just…umm…really attractive."

Now *my* face is burning up. Penny thinks I'm *attractive*?

Her blue-gray eyes lock with mine. "What, you don't get compliments like that?"

LEXI HAYES

I shrug, feeling a surprising vulnerability. "It's, ahh, not the kind of thing I'd expect to hear from a beautiful woman."

The word "beautiful" hangs in the air between us. Penny smiles bashfully and I hurry up and plate our dinners. This girl is rapidly melting my resolve to keep my guard up, and stirring up feelings I *really shouldn't be having*. She only wanted to be nice and deliver some comic books.

Although once I tell her where I've been for the last three years, I'm sure she'll want nothing more to do with me.

CHAPTER 3
PENNY

How did this even happen?

I mean, okay, I know how I got here and how this burly, tattooed mountain man saved me from being eaten alive by the snow. But how does a guy straight out of a rugged bad boy calendar—*who is into comics, for god's sake*—look at *me* like I'm something special?!

I'm short, thick, and a total nerd. That's fine. I own it. I love who I am. It's just… Men with bulging muscles and kind brown eyes rarely give me a second glance.

And… I *think* he and I are flirting? Not that I have much experience with it. But between our playful banter about comic universes and books and my lingering gazes, let's just say I'm frazzled. I blush like crazy whenever he catches me staring. I'm not usually the kind to get this worked up over a guy.

He wouldn't let me help wash the dishes, instead banishing me to the couch with my hot chocolate. It's cozy and warm by the crackling fire and my belly is full after a stellar meal. I'm about to ask him where he learned to cook when my phone pings.

I pull it from my pocket.

How's it going? Please answer or I'll think
you've been chloroformed.

I chuckle and quickly type a reply to JJ.

What if my phone died or I couldn't respond
for some other reason and you sent a SWAT
team for nothing?

Better safe than sorry.

Stop it! I'm fine. Really fine actually. This guy
is...w o w.

W o w ?

He looks like a bearded superhero, and he
made me dinner. Wouldn't even let me help
clean up after!

Probably because he has body parts in his
fridge.

☺ Well, he IS a DC fan.

Even worse!

Please stop worrying. Mitch is a total
gentleman. Though I kinda...wish he wasn't.

omg, Penny!!!

I think I need to start reading more of your
romance collection.

Those are all just fantasies. Fairy tales. You
are in a disturbing situation in REAL LIFE.

Penny: Honestly, I'm totally safe.

Okay, I believe you. For now. But I'm still
staying vigilant.

I put my phone back in my pocket.

"Everything okay?" Mitch calls from the kitchen.

"Yep, JJ's just checking up on me."

"Sounds like a good friend."

"She's the best," I say. "I told her I couldn't talk because my hands were tied, and I had a gag stuffed in my mouth."

I hear him drop a pot in the sink. "Penny..."

"Sorry." I cover my mouth and laugh.

He shakes his head as he comes in bearing a tray of sugar cookies.

"Wait. These are still warm. When did you make them?"

"Just now." He winks. "I whipped up the dough earlier and popped them in just as I started the dishes."

"Sneaky," I say, grabbing one from the tray as he sits down next to me. "But in the best way."

"I didn't have time to ice them, but I figure we can just dunk 'em in our hot chocolate."

Seriously... Who *is* this guy?

"OK, I gotta ask... Where did you learn to do all this?"

"You mean cook?"

"And bake... And take care of strangers you find buried in the snow," I say, dunking my cookie and letting it melt in my mouth.

His smile falters. "A while back my mom got real sick and I had to take care of her and my younger sister. I had to learn this stuff fast."

Oh gosh. "That must've been hard."

19

He nods. "Yeah. It was. Mom passed away a few years back."

"I'm so sorry, Mitch." I put a hand on his knee...and his muscles tense.

"Thanks," he says, glancing down at my hand.

I clear my throat awkwardly. "Is that why you came to Frozen Heights?"

He runs his thumb over the rim of his mug, and I'm almost hypnotized. "Uh... Yeah, I needed a fresh start."

"I can imagine," I finally reply, when I realize he's staring at me. "Where's your sister now?"

The question seems to catch him off guard, and he blinks. "Billings. She's in law school."

"Wow. Good for her."

"Yeah, she's always had a strong moral compass, and a great mind. I'm really proud of her." He looks off across the room and slides away a little.

I pull my hand off his leg. I wish I could touch more of him. Even just to comfort him.

"What about you, Penny?" Mitch's voice is deep and rough, and his rich brown eyes hold mine as he takes a sip of his hot chocolate.

"Well, I guess I told you I work at the Deepwood Library," I start. "But to me, it's more than just a job. I guess I'm kind of obsessed with books and all things tech. I recently graduated and I'm trying to...I dunno, make a difference? It's nothing grand..." My voice trails off, and I realize I'm rambling. It's like his intense gaze can see right through my insecurities.

"Well, you've made a difference for me. Coming all the way out here to deliver comics? You have guts." A playful smirk forms on his rugged face.

"It's all part of my plan," I stammer, taking a deep breath to gather my thoughts. "I love the library, but I want to make it more accessible and fun, you know? Get people excited about reading, especially comic books, and technology. I'm hoping to help create programs that bring those worlds together. Themed events, workshops, maybe even conventions. I really want to make the library the heart of geek culture in Deepwood." As my passion takes over the words flow more smoothly, making me sound less awkward than I feel.

"That sounds amazing, Penny. That's the kind of initiative the world needs more of." His words are kind, and I feel a sense of validation from him, which is strangely comforting. Crap, my face is also heating again.

He grins. "Not to embarrass you even more, but you're really cute when you blush like that."

Oh god! I cover my face with my hands. I'm burning up.

He chuckles. "Sorry... But I'm sure you have tons of guys telling you that every day."

I drop my hands and shoot him an incredulous look. "What? No, never," I admit. "Guys don't usually like me. It's hard to find someone who gets my geekiness, and also...you know...the thick thighs and the stupid freckles don't exactly help."

"That's ridiculous." He peers at me, as if trying to understand the absurdity of my statement. "Believe me, hot, curvy, nerdy girls are *exactly* what a lot of guys dream about. It's just the insecure, clueless ones who'd miss out on a catch like you, Penny."

His words take my breath away. I've never had someone call me hot before, certainly not a man as ruggedly handsome as Mitch.

"Guys are probably just too shy or too nervous to approach you."

Is he even serious right now?

"Th-hanks," I manage to say, swallowing hard. "Um...so... What about you? You have...someone?"

He gives me a crooked smile that has my belly fluttering. "No. I haven't really had the chance to date recently. I'm more focused on getting myself right at the moment."

I nod, taking a sip of my chocolate.

He reaches out. "You've got a little whipped cream right... here." He swipes at my lower lip with his thumb, sending tingles over my skin. I have to hold back from licking it.

I swear he can read my thoughts. He presses his lips together and sits back. "How about we watch a movie?" he suggests, grabbing the remote from the coffee table.

An idea pops into my head, breaking through the lust-filled haze. "Have you seen any of the Marvel movies?"

"Some of the older ones, sure."

"What, have you been under a rock or something the last few years?" I tease.

He bites his lip. "I guess so. I've been...kinda busy."

Oh, right. Dealing with the death of his mom. Way to go, Penny.

"You want to watch one of them?" he asks.

"One? I say we watch *all* of them. A Marvel marathon."

"Now, why would you want to torture the man who just saved you?" he asks, setting his mug down on the coffee table.

I push his shoulder playfully—my god, he's as solid as granite. "You need to see what you're missing, and I'm the perfect tour guide for your journey."

"You think you can convince me to change teams?"

"I know I can!" I say with a grin.

"Fine—you're on," Mitch smiles, and I see a mischievous glint in his eyes.

CHAPTER 4
MITCH

I t's crazy how fate has a way of surprising you, taking an ordinary day in your life and turning it into something extraordinary.

Penny is a tidal wave of energy and passion. As the snow continues to fall outside and we lose ourselves in Marvel's fictional universe, cozied up on the couch together, I'm having a hard time keeping my hands to myself. And I'm not sure how much longer I can hold back.

I also want to tell her the truth about me, to get it out in the open, but I'm scared she'll suddenly see me differently. Worse, that she'll fear me and want to leave.

She insisted on streaming the movies from her phone to my TV in chronological order, starting with *Captain America: The First Avenger.*

Her excitement is childlike and heart-warming, and I'm impressed by her deep knowledge of the Marvel universe when she eagerly points out obscure references and anticipates plot twists—without giving away any spoilers, of course.

I can't help but tease her. "Should I be taking notes? You're making me feel like I'm going to be taking an exam later." I nudge her gently.

Her face lights up in a charming combination of amusement and embarrassment. "I can't help geeking out. This is my happy place." She pauses, her blue-gray eyes sparkling. "Plus, I don't want you to miss out on all the easter eggs!"

I chuckle. "Okay, but just so you know, I *might* blow your mind with some of my theories."

Her eyes get darker and my cock stirs. I think she's as turned on as I am. Maybe.

God, we are *such* nerds.

(I'm loving it.)

I point out plot holes in the storyline, and she counters with intricate explanations as she defends her beloved superheroes. We debate the best and worst adaptations, favorite characters, and the most epic battles.

And I'm *sooo hard*. I'm very thankful the blanket is over my lap.

Every brush of our shoulders or bump of our legs against each other sends a buzz of pleasure through me.

As the second movie, *Captain Marvel*, reaches its climax, Penny's eyes are wide, her attention fully absorbed by the action on screen. "EPIC!" she says. "What do you think, Mitch? You have to admit, this is one of the best battle scenes ever."

"It was pretty damn amazing," I agree, my voice dropping a notch lower as I lean closer to her. "But it's going to take more than that to turn me."

Penny's cheeks flush a delicate pink, and she shoots me a playful grin. "We'll see."

Throughout the second half of the movie, we debate the minutiae of alien ship designs, time travel mechanics, and the psychological complexities of certain characters. Our discussion eases into a more intimate place as we analyze the emotional arcs.

I'm seeing beyond Penny's charming nerdiness and discovering a thoughtful, empathetic woman with a deep-seated desire to understand the world around her. She listens intently as I share my interpretations, considering my opinions with genuine interest.

She sees the real me...not the ex-con, not even the quiet loner.

And she seems like someone who'd accept me for who I am—maybe even love me for it.

The movie finishes and she sighs contentedly as the credits roll, looking utterly satisfied and a little exhausted. "That was intense," she says, blowing out a breath. "You know, I never thought I'd meet someone who'd be up for discussing all the intricate details with me. It's almost..." She trails off and shakes her head, a slight blush creeping up her neck. "Well, it's nice, that's all."

I gaze at her intently. I feel the same way. We just click. "It's fun," I say, "and I appreciate that you get me. A lot of folks think my love for comics and books is kinda strange. It's nice to find someone out there who is the same kind of weird as me."

Penny's sweet face softens, and she reaches over to squeeze my forearm.

I put my hand over hers, staring at her mouth. I want nothing more than to claim those perfect, luscious lips and show her how much I want her. But behind the desire to kiss her lips, taste her skin, and gather her close, losing myself in her softness, is a small voice in the back of my mind reminding me of the big, bad secret I'm keeping from her.

Suddenly the TV screen goes black, and the room is plunged into darkness except for the flickering firelight.

Penny gasps, her hand tensing under mine. "What happened?"

"Power must've gone out." I let go of her, jump up to tend to the fireplace, then move to the window. Through the frosted pane, I can see that the snow is falling harder, and the night is darker and colder than before.

"Shit. That's a real blizzard out there." My brows pull tight with concern. "If this keeps up, we might not get power back for a while."

Penny shivers.

"Cold?" I ask, moving back to sit next to her, my protective instinct immediately rising fiercely.

"A little," she says. That's all it takes for me to pull her against my chest and wrap the blanket around both of us.

"We'll just have to cuddle together here by the fire. I have more than enough wood to last us all weekend." I pause. *Oh god*. "That...came out completely wrong," I backpedal. "I mean, I have more than enough *fire*wood to last us all weekend."

Too late. She's already laughing, her forehead buried in my shoulder.

"That was...bad," I admit. "Sorry."

"Don't be," she says, then snorts, snuggling into the crook of my neck.

Fuck, that's nice.

We stay like that for a moment, the fire's crackling and the storm forming a soothing symphony. My past melts away— my mother's final days, my time in prison—and is replaced by the wonderful here and now. Penny banishes the biting chill of loneliness.

I stroke her back, running my hand up and down to keep her warm. Her soft gasp does all sorts of wicked things to me, sending another rush of blood south, where I'm already aching like crazy. Then her hand comes up to stroke the scruff of my neck, and she lifts her face to mine.

"Penny..." I say in a husky rasp, relishing her body pressed close, her breath hot against my cheek. "I've never wanted someone so bad it fucking hurts before."

She blinks back at me, surprised. "You want *me*?"

"Are you kidding? You're sexy, smart, funny, into tech and comic books! You're my fantasy woman."

Her lips curl into a smile.

She's so fucking adorable. "Do...you want me?"

She nods vehemently. "Yes, yes... *God*, I want you. I just never thought someone like you would be into me."

Penny's breath quickens as I run my nose along her jaw, then gently suck on the pulse point just below her ear. Her sigh is a tantalizing invitation as she turns her face, offering her mouth to me.

I take it, fiercely crushing my lips to hers. Deep inside, past the wanting—past the madness of need burning a path through my veins—I know Penny is mine. She's the light that will guide me back to the life I'm searching for, if my damn secret doesn't screw things up.

She moans into my mouth, and I move down her sweet neck. She shudders, her soft, lush body so precious that it actually makes my chest ache.

All sorts of delicious thoughts course through my mind as I savor the chocolatey taste of her on my tongue. God, I want to ravish her, to strip her naked and worship every glorious, soft inch of her.

I'm claiming her, right here and now.

I pull away momentarily to come up for air. "Why don't we move down to the floor in front of the fire."

CHAPTER 5
PENNY

M itch spreads blankets and cushions out in front of the fire, although I feel like I'm about to combust from the heat already.

Mitch's kiss, his touch, his strong, protective arms wrapped around me… They're are all driving me wild. His muscular frame gently presses against mine, every contour of his chiseled body sending sparks through me. The dancing flames highlight Mitch's rugged features, accentuating the lines of his strong jaw and the intensity of his gaze.

I don't precisely know how we got to this point, but I don't want to stop, despite my reservations.

"You do know you're safe with me, right?" he whispers, his deep voice stoking the fire within me. His words are like a balm soothing my fears and doubts, the ones that always pop up unbidden when I consider how a man, particularly one that looks like Mitch, might feel about me.

I nod, my heart thrumming in my throat. I lean forward, my lips brushing his cheek and his jaw, my breath hitching when I feel the scratchy sensation of his beard against my skin.

My pulse quickens at his groan. "Penny," he rasps, his voice hoarse.

Desire pools low in my belly, and I kiss his sexy mouth.

He makes a sound so raw and full of need that I can't help but whimper. His arms tighten around me, pulling me flush against his hard body. Our kiss deepens, his tongue delving into my mouth hungrily. Desperately. His hand tangles in my hair, holding me in place as he explores my mouth fiercely. I kiss him back just as savagely, gripping his broad shoulders and reveling in the hard planes of his muscles.

Each touch, each taste, is a glimpse into a world I never knew existed—or at least, never thought I'd get to experience. Mitch's rough hands glide over my curves possessively. Urgently. His kisses move from my mouth to my neck, his beard scraping against my heated skin.

Breathless and hungry, I tug up his sweatshirt, needing to feel his skin. Mitch growls, lifting his arms up. A surge of confidence has me gripping the fabric and pulling it completely off over his head, exposing his rugged physique. His body is bulky and thick but sculpted like marble—and I want to make every inch of it shudder with pleasure.

I explore his chest, running my fingers over the ink. "These are incredible," I whisper, tracing the intricate lines of an array of DC characters from Batman to Green Lantern to the Joker.

He shivers at my touch. "You don't think less of me for not having Wolverine?" he asks with a teasing smirk.

I press a kiss to each tattoo, and he groans. "I'll allow it."

"Good to know," he says, his hands moving to my back and sliding under my shirt, pushing it up. "Maybe I can find some of your ink now." His calloused fingers brush against my spine, eliciting a delightful chill.

I grin as he pulls off first my flannel, then my T-shirt. I'm left in my bra. "Keep looking," I say, surprising myself with my boldness.

"Hmmm…" he rumbles, reaching behind me to unhook my bra. He slides the straps down my shoulders and tosses the garment away, lying me down on the rug. His piercing gaze sends a thrilling sense of exposure through me, as if I'm a rare treasure he's just discovered. "Christ, Penny, you're fucking gorgeous," he breathes.

I love hearing him say that in such a rough voice.

He takes both my wrists in one hand and pins them over my head, and I gaze into his intense brown eyes. "I'll have to conduct this search properly," he says, running the knuckles of his free hand down the inside of my arm.

My skin tingles as he drags his fingers over my underarm, skirting the sensitive sides of my breasts. He cups one of them and moves it slightly over and up to peek underneath. "Hmm…nothing yet," he says with a small smile.

He does the same with my other breast, this time rolling his thumb around the peak as my breath stutters. He plays with my nipple, gently tugging it, and I moan.

"Please…more," I whisper.

"Gladly," he groans, lowering to run his tongue over it.

I arch into him, gasping.

Then he sucks my nipple right into his mouth, slowly increasing the force, mimicking the action of his fingers on the other one. I moan loudly.

"Mitch…"

"Feel good, sexy?" he says, in between sucks and kisses.

"Mmm…so good," I reply.

"I'm still looking for those famous tattoos," he says, moving down to kiss my stomach. "May I check here?" he asks, pulling on the button of my jeans.

"God, please do," I groan, and he wastes no time in getting the jeans off me.

"Are these..." He stares at my underwear. "*Iron Man panties?*"

"Um...maybe?"

He chuckles. "Fuck, you're officially my dream girl," he says, and his thumb slides against my pussy. "Damn, Penny, you're soaking Iron Man."

I bite my lip and chuckle along with him.

I stop laughing when he pulls my panties down. "Bingo." He finds the Captain America shield tattoo on my hip. He places a deep, wet kiss over it, and I moan. "Yes sir, Captain sir, I'm gonna make this girl come with my tongue right now."

Oh fuck. I whimper, and he lowers his head, his breath skating along my seam, filling me with anticipation.

"Tell me how much you need my mouth to put out the fire between your sexy thighs."

"I—I feel like I'm going to explode, Mitch. I need you now," I say, running my hands through his hair.

"That's my Supergirl," he says, the heat of his mouth searing against my pussy. When his tongue sweeps along my folds, diving into my slickness, I cry out. I clutch the blanket underneath me as he expertly teases me, making me writhe under him, his mouth finding all my most sensitive spots.

Sparks of pleasure lick at my body. "M-Mitch, oh God, that's..." I gasp, lost for words.

He lifts his head briefly, smiling at me. "You're beautiful when you let go, Penny. Let me hear you. Surrender to me."

He moans against my slick flesh, sending vibrations through my body, his delight in my pleasure intensifying my own arousal.

"I—I can't take any more," I whine, my body rigid with tension. "Please, Mitch. Do it."

"Hell yes, baby," he growls. "Come for me."

His tongue works its magic, tickling my clit. It's all I need to tip me over the edge. A scream tears from my throat as my orgasm explodes, a cascade of sensations and stars bursting behind my eyelids.

"I'm coming, Mitch!" My body trembles and shakes, and he gently continues his exquisite torture until finally I collapse back onto the floor, panting.

He rises and hovers over me, his eyes dark and hungry, and I wrap my arms around him, pulling him close for a searing kiss.

I push him up and flip him over so I'm straddling him. I want to make him feel as good as he made me feel.

"Damn, that's hot," he says, his eyes sparkling, his hands on my legs.

In seconds, I've moved down his brawny body and with impatient hands pulled his sweatpants down and off.

"Baby," he whispers, as my hands discover his thick arousal in his boxers. I stroke him through them, eliciting a hoarse groan of pleasure from deep within his chest.

"Penny," he growls, then bites his lip. "What are you doing to me?"

"I want to taste your cock," I say, encouraging him to lift his hips so I can pull off his boxers as well and get him naked.

"Fucking hell..." he moans.

I'm mesmerized by his cock, so hard and veined, jutting proud before me, the tip already glistening with pre-cum.

Leaning forward, I brush my lips over his length. He lets out a strangled groan, his hands grasping my shoulders and his fingers digging into my skin as I tease him with my tongue, swirling it around the head. I take him into my mouth inch by delicious inch and look up to see his eyes squeezed shut.

"Holy shit," he says, his hand lightly guiding me. "Yeah, that's it. Suck my cock, Penny."

His words scramble my brain. I hollow my cheeks, sucking hard as I pull back, then push forward again, my hand wrapped around the base, stroking in time with my mouth.

Mitch groans my name, his hands spearing through my hair. He thrusts gently into my mouth, meeting my rhythm as if he knows I'm enjoying the power I hold over him.

His scent, a heady mix of musk and smoke, invades my senses, spurring me on. I moan around him, feeling his cock jerk in response.

"*Damn*," he pants, his hips stuttering. "Your mouth...so fucking hot, baby."

His praise has me redoubling my efforts. I slide a hand over his balls to cup and massage them.

With a harsh groan, his hips jerk forward, the tip of his cock hitting the back of my throat. His breath comes in short pants, each thrust growing increasingly erratic.

"I'm close," he grits out. "You're fucking amazing."

His words and the feel of his length sliding over my tongue have my core clenching, and I moan around him.

"Oh...*oh god*, Penny, that's it. I'm coming..." he grunts, emptying himself into my mouth, his hips bucking wildly. I swallow every salty drop eagerly, relishing the taste, milking him with my mouth and hands until he's spent.

CHAPTER 6
MITCH

I sweep Penny into my arms and carry her upstairs to my bedroom, as she guides us with a flashlight.

We're both still naked and she's laughing at my urgency in getting her to bed. I'm aching for her again already...

She's an angel in the warm glow of the candle I light on my bedside table. Her cheeks are flushed from everything we've done tonight. I can't believe this gorgeous creature wants *me*.

"It's cozy up here," she murmurs softly.

"It's about to get even cozier," I reply, my voice turning rougher as my need for her intensifies. I don't know how I can be so hard again, when I just came in her sweet mouth. But I can't get enough of her.

I fumble in the nightstand for a condom before triumphantly grasping the foil wrapper. I take her hand, my large fingers wrapping around her small ones, and tug gently, pulling her closer to me. Bending down, I bury my face in the crook of her neck, inhaling her sweet scent—sugar and spice. My lips brush against her skin, leaving a trail of butterfly kisses up to her earlobe, and she shivers underneath me.

My hands roam over her body, mapping her luscious curves with reverence, exploring her soft skin.

"You're stunning, Penny," I breathe, my voice hoarse as I gaze down at her. Her breasts rise and fall rapidly, her breath mingling with mine. I lean over, capturing a dusky peak in my mouth and sucking. Her moan of approval has my cock leaking with pre-cum. I worship her body with kisses, lavishing attention on each curve and hollow.

"Mitch, please," she pleads. "I need you inside me."

I grin into her collarbone, thrilled that she's just as eager and needy as I am.

"Take what you want, then," I say, capturing her face in my hands, looking deep into her lust-filled eyes. "Take control. Show me how much you want this."

She needs no further encouragement. With a gleam in her eyes, she pushes me onto my back and then straddles my waist. Her hands skim over my chest, her thumbs brushing my nipples, and I groan. She leans forward to trail kisses down my neck, her nails dragging along my stomach, coaxing anxious sounds from deep within my throat.

I tear open the condom wrapper and hand it to her, watching in awe as she rolls it onto my throbbing length, her hair falling forward in a seductive tease over her face.

Then she lifts herself up to position her thick, lush body over my cock. We both let out a groan as she lowers herself onto me, enveloping me in her wet heat, welcoming me in with a slow, almost tortuous, descent.

"God, you feel incredible," I moan, my eyes fluttering shut.

Penny experiments with her movements, rising and falling, grinding and swiveling her hips to discover what gives us both the most pleasure. The sight of her above me, her long hair cascading down her back, her eyes dark with desire, her full, round tits swaying, fuels my burning need.

"Tell me what you want. I'll give it to you," I growl.

She bites her lip, her expression suddenly coy. "I want to feel you come, Mitch," she whispers. "I want to ride you, feel you filling me with your cum and claiming every inch of my body."

Her dirty talk sets my blood on fire. "Damn it, Penny." I cup her big breasts, squeezing. "Then that's what I'll do. I'm going to fill you up, claim you, and come...just for you. Only for you."

Her eyes flash and she moves slowly at first, getting used to my size, then sets a pace that has me digging my heels into the mattress. "Yes, Penny," I hiss, my body coiled with tension. "That's it, baby."

Her smile is wicked as she moans loudly, throwing her head back.

Watching her in ecstasy shatters my control, and I grip her hips, holding her in place as I thrust up, meeting her descending body, driving us both toward our climax.

"Mitch!" Penny screams, her voice high-pitched, body tensing as the tidal wave of her orgasm crashes over her. I watch, mesmerized, as she surrenders.

I should come, but not yet. I need to see that again. Need to bring her to that peak once more. I guide her through the ripples of her climax, pulling her down to capture her lips as I continue to move within her, picking up the pace once again.

She responds eagerly, meeting my rhythm, her heavy tits bouncing, our bodies slapping together wetly.

"I'm close," I grind out. "I'm coming with you this time, sweetheart."

She nods fiercely, her gaze locked on mine, and she swallows hard, visibly working to let me catch up. "Mitch, I—" she pants, her words punctuated by the pounding of our bodies.

My thumb finds her clit, rubbing gently, until I feel her

body tremble. "Oh god..." she moans. "Mitch, it feels so damn good."

"It sure does," I say, about to sail over the edge. "Now, let go. I've got you. Come with me."

Her pussy clamps down on me hard and I detonate, grabbing onto her. Together, we soar, crying out each other's names, sweat-slicked bodies sliding over each other. I feel Penny in every fiber of my being, every nerve ending, and deep within my heart.

This brilliant woman, this passionate soul, is the one for me. And I claim her with all the ferocity I possess.

"M-mine," I stammer, my voice thick, my eyes closing in euphoric exhaustion.

As our heartbeats slow and our breathing returns to normal, I pull Penny down onto my chest. Her hand rests over my heart, a soothing caress that calms the storm within.

"Penny, I've never felt this way before. So alive, so complete."

Penny lifts her head, her eyes searching mine, lips curving into a soft smile. "Mitch, I—I know it's fast, and it's going to sound crazy, but I feel like I've waited my whole life for you." She rests her head against my chest, her hand squeezing mine where they're entwined beneath us.

I tighten my hold on her, a shudder of deep emotion wracking my body. "I'm keeping you, Penny. You're mine to cherish and protect and worship. My everything." Pulling back slightly, I tilt her chin up and kiss her, sealing the unspoken promise between us. "I love you. With everything I am and ever will be."

Penny's eyes shine, her smile equally radiant as she brushes her fingers through my beard. "And I love you, too, Mitch."

I should tell her. Right the hell now. About my mom's

medical bills, my desperation that led to me burglarizing those homes, and my time in prison.

But god, it feels good to know she loves me. This amazing creature loves me.

And once I tell her, that might all change.

I'll tell her tomorrow morning. First thing.

For now, I just want to pretend we're two souls forever destined to be together who have finally found each another.

CHAPTER 7
PENNY

A s the morning light starts to peek through the cabin's windows, I wake up in a cocoon of blankets. I'm alone but can hear the sound of running water. Mitch must be in the shower.

Snowflakes drift lazily past the glass as I remember last night—the way we kissed, touched, and made love...god, so many times. But we also connected on another level...through our love of reading, of comics, and life passions. It was like something straight out of one of JJ's romance novels.

How else could I have fallen for someone so quickly? I mean, I don't even really know the man.

I roll over, my entire body sore in the best possible way.

After we fell asleep, we woke up later to do it all over again, except this time Mitch took me from behind, finding the rest of my Marvel tattoos in the process—the Scarlet Witch on my ankle, the Black Widow on my shoulder, and the Avengers logo on my lower back—and making me come twice more with his skilled hands and impressive cock.

I swell with pride, thinking back to his words in my ear telling me I was driving him mad with lust. And when he gasped and moaned, and finally roared when he climaxed, I nearly came myself, knowing I was making this big, brawny man lose all control.

Men have always confused me. But something about this mountain man with a kind heart has shattered any walls I had, leaving me exposed and craving more. My heart pounds with excitement as I think about a future with him.

Then I glance at my phone.

There's a text from JJ.

> Penny, I did some digging. Mitch Brooks is fresh out of prison. For burglary. Be careful, okay? I don't want you getting hurt.

My hands shake as I read the message—once, twice, three times.

What?

JJ must have guessed that something was fishy; she always has a sixth sense about these things.

But prison? Burglary? *Really?*

Why didn't he tell me? He had plenty of time to.

My mind whirls with hurt, anger...sadness. Surprisingly, I'm not afraid. I somehow know Mitch isn't someone to fear. Mainly, I'm upset that he kept it from me. But even as that pricks my heart, another huge part of me wants to understand and give him the benefit of the doubt.

Not right now, though. I'm way too hurt to think straight.

I get up from the bed, a mess of nerves. I get dressed quickly and check outside. The snow is light, and most of it has melted since last night. I can easily see my pickup.

I hear the shower stop and I push open the bathroom door just as he's wrapping a towel around his waist.

Damn... Why does he have to be so flipping sexy? Broad and muscled, with tons of delicious ink. Water droplets roll

40

down his skin, and I fight the urge to follow them with my tongue.

"You're dressed already?" His brow lifts, surprise on his face.

"I'm leaving," I say, then clear my throat. "JJ tells me you were in prison."

"Penny, I—" Mitch begins, his eyes searching mine.

"Save it." I cut him off, my voice shaking. "How can I trust you, Mitch? You let me believe you were something you weren't when I bared everything to you, especially my heart. For all I know, you were lying about last night, too. I—I thought we had something special… Now I'm not so sure."

Mitch steps closer, his gaze fixed on me intently, and for a second, I lose myself in those deep, piercing eyes. I shake it off and take a step away.

"Please, Penny, just let me explain," he pleads, his voice quiet but desperate. "I never wanted to hurt you. I wanted to tell you everything last night, but I was afraid of scaring you away. I just got out a couple months ago, and I'm trying to start over."

I feel my resolve cracking and my anger softening as I see the vulnerability in his eyes. But I push the feelings down, not wanting to be swayed by his charms or his ludicrously handsome face.

"Yeah, well, instead you betrayed my trust…and it hurts more than I thought it would," I say firmly, turning to go. "I need some time to think. But not here. Not… Not so close to you."

His face falls, pain and regret etched on his gorgeous features. "I—I respect that. But please, know that everything I said, everything I feel for you is real. If you let me, I'll prove it to you. Just give me a chance to make this right."

"We'll see," I reply. Without another word, I head downstairs and out into the cold morning air. As I get into my car, I see him standing at his bedroom window, watching me, looking just as lost and heartbroken as I feel.

As I go through the motions at the Deepwood Mountain Library on Monday morning, I can't shake this totally surreal feeling. It's as if I'm watching a movie of someone else's life instead of living my own. The voices of my boss and colleagues, the familiar chirps and beeps of the library computer systems, the endless lines of code, none of it seems… right…after spending the night with Mitch. I keep glancing at my phone, half-expecting a message from him, but the stupid thing remains stubbornly silent.

Well. I *did* tell him to give me some time. I guess I should be glad he's respecting my wishes.

But *god*, it would be amazing to hear his deep voice and be held in his powerful arms right now.

I cried and moped all weekend, dragging poor JJ into the whole sorry mess. She listened to me rant and rave. She didn't judge me, either. Surprisingly, she didn't say anything bad about Mitch—just let me get it all off my chest.

My thoughts continue to drift back to him and to everything we shared. The Mitch I met—the tattooed giant who loves DC comics and makes me feel like the most special woman in the world—was it all an act?

Can I trust someone who's willing to hide the truth even if he claims to love me?

"Delivery," JJ says, as she walks into the IT offices carrying a beautiful bouquet of wildflowers in hues of blue and red, a small, sealed gold envelope buried in them.

"Wow." My boss Hawk adjusts his glasses as he looks up from his computer. "Does Penny finally have a suitor?"

"Suitor?" I say, furrowing my brow. "How old *are* you, like ninety?"

JJ stifles a giggle and Hawk narrows his eyes. "Watch it! I'll have Willa put you on inventory checks of your least favorite genres for the rest of the week."

"Okay, I take it back," I say hastily, chuckling. "You're not old. But *suitor*? Really?"

He rolls his eyes, and I inhale the sweet scent of the flowers JJ places on my desk.

"Gee, I wonder who these could be from?" she asks with a wink.

My heart is fluttering as I open the card and my hands are trembling, eager yet afraid of what it might say.

My Sweet Penny,

From the moment I saw your beautiful, freckled face, your blue-gray eyes and your genuine smile, I knew I had to make you mine. You're a warm flame on a cold night, so full of life, and you're everything I've ever wanted in a woman. In a partner.

I held back from telling you the truth about my past because I thought it would ruin us before we even got started. It was selfish. I was thinking only of protecting myself from the hurt of rejection.

Being in prison changes a person. It's made me guarded and afraid to let people in. But for some reason it seems the most natural thing in the world for me to let you in. And I truly never meant to deceive you.

Please let me apologize. I can only imagine the thoughts running through your mind right now, and you deserve an explanation—one I would like to give you in person.

What we have is special and I won't let my past mistakes take away the best thing that's ever happened to me. That's you, Penny. I'm willing to do whatever it takes to earn back your trust. Even if it means waiting patiently—I'm good at that—for you to give me another chance.

Love always,

Mitch

P.S. I'd even give up DC and go over to the dark side of Marvel for you. But only for you.

Tears blur my vision, and I feel a lump forming in my throat. Part of me just wants to be done with him and move on, like it never happened. But the rest of me has been charmed by him, and his words tug at the heartstrings he reached in and took a hold of so easily.

"You okay?" JJ asks. "What did Mitch say?"

0

"Wait, who's Mitch?" Hawk asks.

"Her *suitor*," JJ announces with a smirk.

I shake my head. "He wants a chance to explain himself and apologize to me in person."

"Sounds fair," JJ says. "You deserve that. Why don't you have him meet you here at the end of the day. That way me and Hawk can keep an eye on him."

I fix Hawk and JJ with a look. "Only if you two promise to behave yourselves."

They both look at one another innocently, like it's ridiculous to think they'd be anything other than perfectly pleasant.

Still... I *know* them.

"Hawk can be our backup if Mitch tries anything," JJ says, and Hawk's eyes go wide.

"Wait a minute...how big *is* this guy?" He crosses his arms over his chest and squints at me. "And why would he be *trying* anything?"

"She's *joking*, Hawk," I say. "He's not going to try anything. Don't worry about it."

But JJ helpfully adds, "Think as tall as you, but ripped and with tats." Thankfully, she leaves out the prison thing.

"JJ, stop!" I order, chuckling as Hawk tugs on his collar a little.

I pull out my phone and text Mitch at the number he wrote on the card, telling him to meet me at the library at closing.

My message gets a swift response.

I'll be there, Penny. Grateful for the chance. 🩶

How is this man melting my heart already?

Still, as the end of the day approaches, my anxiety mounts.

When Mitch strides into the library, his imposing figure draws the attention of everyone present, including me. In

45

jeans, coat, and hat, he's even sexier than I remember. And every intimate thing that we did slams into me. I'm about to run over and jump into his arms when Hawk and JJ move in front of me.

As Mitch walks up to the front desk, Hawk mutters, "Shit, is this him? He's a damn brick house." Still, Hawk stands tall and greets him. "Evening, sir. We're about to close for the day. Is there something I can quickly help you with?"

"I'm…um…looking for Penny. She asked me to meet her here."

I step forward, coming around JJ and up next to Hawk. "It's fine, Hawk. I'm going to take Mitch to Study Room 1 to talk for a few minutes, if that's okay."

I grab Mitch's big, calloused hand and lead him quickly to the study room.

Closing the door behind us, I turn to him. "Sorry I didn't introduce you. Hawk and JJ were being a little overprotective earlier."

"Hawk?"

I nod. "He's my boss. The girl in the cardigan is JJ."

He smiles. "I'm glad you have people looking out for you," he says, his eyes on our intertwined hands. "Penny," he starts, his voice husky. "Thank you for giving me the chance to explain myself." His brown eyes, usually so warm and inviting, are now full of remorse.

I see the raw emotion etched on his rugged face, and my heart constricts. "I'll listen to your explanation, Mitch, but I swear, if you ever keep something from me again, I won't be so understanding."

Mitch nods, his eyes closing briefly as if steeling himself. "I promise. I know I messed up, and I'll spend the rest of our lives making it up to you…if you'll let me."

I nod, smiling up at him. "All right, explain yourself."

He sighs. "When mom got sick, there was no one to take care of her. My sister Kendra offered to drop out of high school, but I wouldn't let her. She was the one with all the brains. I knew she had the talent to do big things in this world. So I dropped out of college and got a job in construction to pay the bills.

"Whenever I wasn't working, I was taking care of both of them. But Mom got to the point where she needed around-the-clock care. I didn't have the money to put her in a nice facility. The ones I *could* afford were shitholes—not to mince words, sorry. How could I let the woman who had done everything for us live out the rest of her days in a place like that?

"My only option was to find the money for a good place any way I could. I cased the most affluent neighborhoods in Billings and began burglarizing people's homes when they were out. Big ticket items that were mere luxuries for these people and probably insured anyway. I did that for months, allowing my mom to live out her remaining days with the best possible care.

"Luckily, Mom passed shortly before they caught me, so she never knew. My face mask slipped on my last hit and one of the security cameras clocked me. I was given a pretty lenient sentence, all things considered. I guess the judge sympathized with my situation. But my sister has never forgiven me. She understands why I did it, but as a budding lawyer with a very black and white moral code, she's made it clear she doesn't want anything to do with me."

He brings my hand up to his lips and kisses it. "When I got out I... I never expected to meet someone like you, Penny. My heart has never felt so full, and I want to show you every day that you can trust me with yours."

I'm speechless.

I can't even imagine going through what he had and

making it through to the other side with such clarity and grace.

"Can I—can *we* start over?" he whispers. "Give me a chance to show you who I am—the man underneath the tattoos and the prison record?"

My heart pounds, and all I want to do is feel his big strong arms around me. "You are an amazing man, Mitch. A real superhero. So what if your back story is a little complicated? I can't wait to get to know everything about you—the good, the bad, and the in-between."

I jump into his arms and he holds me tight against him. "But no more secrets, mister. Ever," I whisper in his ear, inhaling his fresh scent—like powdery snow and pine trees.

"I promise," he vows, stroking my hair. "Just us, together, building something real and honest."

His mouth captures mine, and I respond eagerly, our kiss a storm of pent-up emotion and relief. We draw apart, breathless, and I see my own determination and hope reflected in his rich brown eyes.

EPILOGUE - MITCH

ONE YEAR LATER

A s I step out back, the anticipation of the moment finally hits me. My heart, seasoned with life's challenges, thunders with nerves and sheer excitement.

I'm about to marry my soulmate...my Penny...in the heart of Deepwood Mountain, in the little park behind the Community Hall.

It's a day I never imagined would come, and now it's unfolding like the sweetest of dreams.

The comic book-themed decor, the ice sculptures of our favorite characters, and the buffet featuring food from various fandoms blend seamlessly with the natural beauty of the mountainside.

I'm dressed as Penny's favorite male superhero, Captain America. It took about seven months to get in good enough shape that I felt comfortable wearing the tight-fitting costume with a star at the center of my chest. But I did it. And I have to admit, today, I look *bad-ass*.

But as good as I might look, Penny blows me out of the water. Naturally. She's always gorgeous, even in just sweats and T-shirt, but dressed as my favorite female superhero,

Wonder Woman...damn. Her breasts are barely contained by the blue bodice that cinches in at her waist, and her generous ass teases me in the red form-fitting bottoms. Fortunately, my cock is *seriously* locked down in my own outfit to save me any embarrassment in front of our friends and family.

I smile when I spot my sister, Kendra. She surprised us when she RSVPed that she would attend. She mentioned wanting to talk, and I'm very thankful for her willingness to do so. JJ is standing up at the front with us as Penny's maid of honor, and my cousin Conner, who flew in from the East Coast, is acting as my best man. Hawk and a few people from the library are here, and a lot of Penny's family. Her father gave her away and her mother is already dabbing at her eyes in the front row.

A gentle breeze rustles through the trees, the early spring air carrying the scent of fresh wildflowers and pine. The breathtaking backdrop of snow-capped mountains and towering trees surrounds our wedding venue. I gaze at Penny and think for the millionth time how lucky I am.

Just as the nerves threaten to take over, I hear the resonant voice of the officiant. It's the new priest from the local church, Father Nathan, who's become a great friend and was happy to perform the ceremony outside here. He stands at the wooden arch adorned with holly and winter blooms, his warm smile encouraging us both.

"Ladies and gentlemen, geeks and non-geeks alike, we are gathered here today to celebrate a love that defies all odds," Nate begins. "We're here to witness a union not just of two people but of two worlds, where the might of DC meets the magic of Marvel." The crowd erupts in laughter and cheers.

"Our groom, Mitch, has requested to go first in his vows. Eager as always," he continues, winking. I step forward, taking a moment to appreciate the woman who has changed my life. I can't believe this incredibly smart, funny, and beauti-fully nerdy woman is my bride.

I take her hands in mine. "Penny, meeting you was a plot twist I never saw coming. You stormed into my solitary world, a whirlwind of passion, energy, and relentless spirit. You braved a snowstorm to bring me those comics and I instantly knew you were a lot more than just a sweet library support tech. You're…kinda crazy." I pause at the chuckles in the audi-ence, a hint of pink staining Penny's cheeks. "Your boundless heart has taught me that love can be just around every corner, even in the remotest of places."

My voice grows thick with emotion as I continue. "I pledge always to be your protector, your confidant, and your partner in this wild adventure. I'll feed your passions, encourage your dreams, and embrace your fierce spirit with my own. Together, we will vanquish any challenge, be it an evil supervillain or the treacherous path of everyday life. With you, I've found home—not just in this mountain range, but in your embrace. And I'll always love you."

There's a collective happy sigh from the crowd, followed by light laughter and one or two hoots. Penny, wiping a tear from her eye, takes her turn to speak. I squeeze her hand as she trembles.

"Mitch, from the moment I first saw you, a towering moun-tain of a man carrying me through a snowstorm, I felt some-thing raw and fierce stir within me, unlike anything I've known." She pauses, her eyes locking with mine, and my heart skips. "You were like a secret hidden beneath the ice, waiting to be discovered. Beneath your rough exterior, I found the heart of a hero, a man prepared to sacrifice everything for his family."

Penny smiles. "You've shown me the true strength of a man —not just through muscles and force, but through love, empathy, and unwavering dedication. You've embraced my world of fandoms, technology, and dreams, and now I've found a home in your heart."

Taking a deep breath, Penny concludes, "I stand here not as the shy, awkward girl who stumbled upon your solitude, but as your equal, ready to face the world and create a life of joy. I vow to love you, support you…and always to challenge you in our Marvel vs. DC debates!" Laughter and cheers erupt in the crowd.

We squeeze each other's hands, and the ceremony concludes with the exchange of rings, securing the promises spoken between us. The rings are engraved with our favorite quotes from our respective fandoms. I slip the simple silver band onto Penny's finger, and then she does the same for me. A surge of happiness washes through me as I see our hands together.

Nate, beaming, announces, "By the power vested in me by God, the state of Montana, and the ever-present force of geek-dom, I pronounce you husband and wife. Mr. and Mrs. Brooks, you may seal your vows with a kiss."

The past year, filled with growth, trust, and discovery, flashes before my eyes. From our first encounter in the snow, it's been a whirlwind journey that has changed me forever. And now we confirm our destiny with a kiss, passionate and sweet—a kiss that signifies new beginnings and the creation of a home within each other.

As I pull Penny to me tightly, deepening our kiss, laughter and applause ring out all around us. I pull back slightly, gazing into Penny's sparkling eyes, and whisper, "You're all mine, Mrs. Brooks."

The festivities continue late into the night, with toasts, dances, and even a spontaneous Marvel vs. DC trivia contest.

Penny and I steal away to take a private moment under the

glow of the full moon. Bundled in my arms, she sighs, her breath visible in the crisp air. "I can't believe this is our life now, Mitch. Our own fairy tale in the mountains."

I nuzzle her neck. "I can. I staked my claim the moment I pulled you from the snow and held you in my arms."

She chuckles and cups my face in her hands. "My hero," she whispers, and my heart melts.

TRAPPED WITH THE GROWLY ROCK STAR

CHAPTER 1
HALLIE

"Come on, June, it's not like I'm asking you to help me rob a bank or stave off a zombie apocalypse. I just want the smallest piece of information." I give my best friend a pleading smile as I lean forward, resting my elbows on the dispatch desk.

She bites her lip. I know her. That means she's considering my request. "Isaac will legit kill me if he finds out I told you where Lennox Steele is staying in Frozen Heights."

"But he won't find out. Not if you keep your mouth shut." I waggle my eyebrows hopefully.

"You know how hard it is for me to keep *anything* from him," she groans.

"Yeah, because he threatens you with a spanking, and you cave," I say, with a laugh. "And then he spanks you anyway."

"Hallie!" she shrieks, her cheeks turning pink.

"Hey, you think I like knowing that about my boss?" Not just my boss: Sheriff Quinn and I have known each other since I was a baby. Ugh. I shudder. TMI.

I should mention that tracking down Lennox Steele—the legendary rock star who's been off the radar for years now—

isn't important to me personally. But getting his autograph would mean the world to my little sister, his biggest fan. And Ciara's been through a lot this year with her health issues.

So if an autograph makes her smile…? It's worth every risk.

"Okay, fine," Juniper says at last. "But only because Ciara's my favorite kid in Deepwood, aside from my own. And you better believe I want to hear that her face lit up brighter than the tree when she opens that present on Christmas morning." She pokes a finger in my chest. "*And* if my husband finds out, I'll say you blackmailed me, and there'll be hell to pay." She's only half-joking. Sheriff Quinn has an overprotective streak, and he'd never let either of us out of his sight if he knew what we were up to.

"Eee! Thank you. Love you, Juney." I tackle her and give her a big kiss on the cheek.

She giggles and extricates herself, grabbing my phone off the desk. "Just be careful," she says, typing in Lennox's cabin address. "The weather forecast isn't looking great, and you know how unpredictable these mountain storms can be." Her blue eyes are serious. "And I hope you remember that Lennox Steele has a reputation for being an asshole…" She trails off, not needing to enumerate the various tales of his stints in rehab and preference for privacy.

"Yes. And I appreciate your concern, but I've got this. Lennox might be a bit of a grouch, but I bet he can't resist a redhead in a Sheriff's Department polo and tactical pants." I strike a sultry pose for her.

Juniper chuckles, shaking her head. "Let's hope you're right. Please, *please* don't do anything stupid and make me regret letting you go alone."

"You've got two little ones that need their mama safe at home. I'm a big girl. I can handle myself. I promise to be extra careful."

She crosses her arms. "Yeah. I've heard that before."

"But I mean it this time," I reply with a smirk. She rolls her eyes.

I zip up my coat, give her another hug and final wave goodbye, and set off for the remote peaks of Frozen Heights. As I travel up the mountainside, the air grows colder even inside my heated Jeep, and the wind howls, almost as if the mountains themselves are warning me of the challenges ahead.

But ultimately the ride to the base of Frozen Heights is uneventful, and I make good time.

An hour later, after navigating steep inclines and dense forests on either side of the road, I finally catch sight of my destination: a modern luxury cabin nestled among the towering snow-covered pines, smoke curling from the chimney. It looks like the most inviting place in the world right now, but I know better than to expect a warm welcome.

I park and trudge through the snow toward the front. My body warms with each step, the physical effort required nothing when I imagine Ciara's eyes sparkling with joy when she opens the signed photograph from her idol.

I ring the fancy doorbell and knock on the massive door, then wait.

No response.

I repeat it all again, this time calling out, "Hello? Mr. Steele? I'm here with the Sheriff's Department." It's not remotely official business, but I figure that could help stir some urgency.

Still nothing.

"Great. He's either not home or ignoring me," I mumble to myself, frustrated. "Guess it's time for Plan B."

I start making my way around the house, getting as close as I can to peek in the windows. I don't see anyone on the first floor. But it would be great to check the second floor, too. I scan the area and spot a tall, thick pine tree a few feet from the cabin.

Perfect.

I approach the tree and begin climbing. The height will give me a better view of the cabin and, hopefully, proof he's home and a chance to catch his attention.

As I climb, the wind picks up and the snow starts falling even more thickly. Hmm. Climbing trees was a lot easier when I was a little kid. At 24, I'm not quite as spry, or unbreakable. This *might* be one of those stupid things Juniper warned me not to do. But eventually I reach a suitable branch and perch there, feeling quite proud of myself.

The curtains are open, and I can see almost the entirety of the top floor.

That's when Lennox Steele walks right into my view.

Stark. Flipping. Naked.

Holy shit.

The man is a work of art...and the chef's kiss of rugged sex appeal.

He's got to be in his late forties now, but my god, his body is still as chiseled as that of a man half his age. Broad shoulders, bulky pecs, just the right amount of hair trailing down his chest, his abs, and dropping between that muscled "V".

As if that hasn't scrambled my brain enough, my gaze zeroes in on his enormous...umm...

Wow. Is he ever *blessed*.

His hair is wet, like he's just come from the shower.

Then he stretches.

It's a full-body stretch that flexes all his delicious muscles, putting everything on display. Oh, lord!

Suddenly I'm burning up despite the blizzard. I actually have to bite my lip to stop from gasping.

"Hallie, focus," I mutter, closing my eyes for a moment. "You're here for Ciara, not to stare at a naked and very well-hung rock star."

Then I sneak another peek. I mean, I'm only human.

He's now sitting on his bed holding a guitar, his long, skilled fingers plucking the strings with a strange expression on his face...part passion, part frustration. He sings—and though I can't actually hear him, I can imagine his voice in my head—rough, raw, and soulful. I'm captivated. I can understand why Ciara adores him.

A snapping sound jolts me back to reality.

Oh no...

The branch I'm sitting on snaps again, this time giving way, and suddenly I'm falling straight down into—thankfully—a mound of snow below. Still, the impact knocks the wind out of me, and I lie there, temporarily stunned.

"Ow, that's gonna leave a mark," I groan, assessing the situation. Slowly, I lift my head, chilled to the bone, gingerly trying to gauge the damage. I'm sore, and probably bruised, but it doesn't feel like anything's sprained or broken.

Still, if I don't get back to my Jeep soon, I'm going to freeze to death.

As I prepare to sit up, I'm lifted up almost effortlessly by a strong pair of arms.

"What the hell are you doing out here?" a deep, rumbling voice says near me. I find myself staring up into the most intense gray eyes I've ever seen. His voice is gravelly, like his vocal cords have been roughed up by sandpaper, and his lips are pressed into a hard line. It's *him*. Lennox Steele. Up close and personal.

"Well?" he adds impatiently when I don't answer right away. Okay, he's kinda grumpy.

"I...um..." I stutter, my brain scrambling for an excuse. "I...

I'm so sorry. I didn't mean... I was..." My face heats up as I trail off, cursing my fumbling words under his piercing gaze. I've seen a lot of things in my day—crazy car accidents, bear attacks, you name it—but nothing has left me as tongue-tied as this man's smoldering eyes.

"We don't have all day, honey. We'll freeze our asses off out here. Are you okay to stand?"

I nod. "You're Lennox Steele," I blurt, my mind still a jumble.

"Yeah. And who are you?" He hauls me to my feet, and I realize he's now wearing sweats and a huge parka with a fur-lined hood.

"I-I'm Hallie Owens," I manage to say. Who knew I'd get so starstruck?

"Can you walk?"

I nod again. Words are *incredibly* difficult to find when this man is next to me.

"Then let's get our butts inside. I can't feel my goddamn face," he snaps, wrapping his arm around me and leading me through the storm.

When we make it into the cabin, he removes his parka and boots, then helps me with my coat.

"Sheriff's Department?" he asks, glancing down at the logo on my polo shirt. "Go sit by the fire and grab a blanket from the sofa. Warm yourself up," he orders. "Then tell me what's going on, Ms. Owens."

"Call me Hallie," I say, doing as I'm told.

The fireplace is massive, the sofa something straight out of a design magazine. I sit and remove my boots and wet socks as he leaves the room.

Lennox returns with two coffees and hands one to me. Our fingers brush, sending shivers through me that have nothing to do with the residual cold from the snow.

He sits next to me in a T-shirt and sweatpants, looking like a dream.

Except for that stupid scowl on his face.

"Let's hear it, Hallie," he says sternly, and my name in that rough voice sends pools of heat straight to my core, despite his gruff tone. "What is someone from the Sheriff's Department doing out here?"

I take a deep breath, pulling the blanket tighter around my shoulders. "I need your autograph."

If I thought he was scowling before, now he's livid.

"You risked your life, falling from a fucking tree in the middle of a blizzard, for an *autograph*?"

"Yes, but—"

"Unbelievable," he scoffs, looking away. "Okay, once you get warmed up and finish your coffee, you need to leave. I should report you to the Sheriff himself. He gave me his word no one would know I was even here."

"Please don't, Mr. Steele," I begin, my heart sinking. "He knows nothing of this. I found out on my own. I can be pretty ingenious when I want something."

"So, stalking then?" he supplies dryly.

"Not stalking..." One of his dark eyebrows quirks up skeptically. "Not *completely*." I sit up straighter. Crap. This is not how I envisioned this meeting would go, but I'm not one to back down easily. "I swear, if you want me to leave empty-handed, I will. But I had to try. The autograph's not for me, it's for my little sister, Ciara. She's your biggest fan. She has JIA—chronic arthritis—and she's had a *really* shitty year. I heard you were in town, and I guess I hoped I could make her Christmas special with an autograph from her idol."

A flash of different emotions—surprise, wariness, maybe mixed with a smidge of sympathy—crosses Lennox's rugged features. He considers my words, his gruff exterior softening for a moment. "I'm sorry she's had a rough year," he murmurs quietly. "Sure. I'll sign something for your sister. But then you go on your way."

Relief washes over me. "Oh, thank you so much, Mr. Steele! Ciara's going to flip—"

He waves me off. "Call me Lennox. Mr. Steele sounds like some vintage superhero, and I'm anything but that."

I smile as he gets up to leave the room. "Back in a minute."

While he's gone, I look around curiously. The interior of the cabin is modern and luxurious, but it's clearly a rental. The artwork on the walls is bland without any hint of personality. The only clue that a musician is staying here is the array of guitars—both acoustic and electric—scattered about, some music manuscript paper on chairs and side tables, and a keyboard set up so that when you play you face the huge floor-to-ceiling windows near the back of the house overlooking the snow-covered mountainside.

…The mountainside that is currently getting pummeled with snow. It's piling up along the side of the house and the sky is crazy dark. Oh man. How am I going to get home in *that*?

I'm taking a nervous sip of my coffee when Lennox returns with an old vinyl album of his and a pen.

He sits down next to me on the couch, tucking a long leg underneath him. "How do you spell your sister's name?"

"C-i-a-r-a," I say, as he scribbles something on the cover. Then he hands it to me.

My heart throbs as I take it. I recognize it as his debut album, Ciara's favorite. "She'll love it," I murmur, running my fingers over the cover. "This will make her Christmas. Thank you again." I look up to see him studying me with intense eyes.

"Even though I'm not condoning your methods, you took a

risk for someone you love and I respect that. Not many people would have braved these conditions, even if it was for a very good cause." He pauses. "Fame has taught me that kindness from others usually comes with a price."

His words hang in the air, heavy and bitter. This man who once had the world at his feet now seems defeated, a mere shadow of the icon he once was. But I think I still see a hint of the fire that burned so brightly before in his smoldering eyes.

"That's too bad. I know I'd do *anything* for my family and friends. And as a proud member of the Sheriff's Department, I risk a lot for other people...for nothing in return."

He doesn't answer, so I get ready to leave. I know I'm in danger of overstaying my welcome any second.

Just then, a gust of wind slams into the cabin.

We both jump and turn to look out the windows.

Everything is white. The sky, the trees, the ground. You can barely make out the shapes of anything.

"I made gumbo," he grunts, turning back to me. "You might as well grab a bowl for dinner. Doesn't look like you're going anywhere for a while."

CHAPTER 2
LENNOX

I pace the confines of my cabin, feeling like a caged animal. The snowstorm raging outside only mirrors the chaos of white noise within me.

This damn creative block is killing me. My deadline is looming larger and larger, and I'm no closer to penning a hit than I was when I first arrived at this godforsaken place.

Frozen Heights…more like Frozen Hell.

I shake my head, trying to clear my mind and ignore the frustration simmering inside me. My daily routine has become a repetitive cycle of self-inflicted torture. I wake up, force myself to hold my dad's old Gibson acoustic, and stare at the blank notepad, willing something…anything…to come. Some days, I scribble down a few meaningless notes and phrases before crumpling the paper in disappointment. Others I don't even bother, instead wandering listlessly around the cabin, or sitting in the armchair by the fireplace staring at the flames, wishing they'd consume me once and for all.

The silence here is supposed to be therapeutic, but it's driving me insane. I miss the chaos of being in the studio, the buzz of ideas bouncing off the walls, feeding off the energy of others. But I lost almost all my work contacts, friends, and even family years ago from my addiction to alcohol. I think my manager, Wally, only sticks with me because he's nutty enough to believe I'll be back on top again one day, making him rich.

It's left me alone with my demons. Not the ones I booted to get sober, but the ones that continually whisper I'm way past my prime.

I take a hot shower, then walk into my bedroom and stretch, taking a big, deep lungful of this mountain air. Even with all the snow, I like to keep the window cracked open. I grab the Gibson and sit on the bed, strumming aimlessly. This instrument, once my trusted companion, now feels foreign and unfamiliar. And silent.

I've been away for five years, which is officially a lifetime for a musician. My last album, *Soul's Farewell*, was a farewell to more than just my life as I knew it back then—it apparently marked the end of my creative flow, leaving me hollow and empty. Once, I could seduce thousands and come up with endless melodies and lyrics, but now, even a single verse feels beyond me.

Cradling the guitar close to my body, I try a few broken words, then curse under my breath.

"Focus. Prove everyone wrong, especially yourself," I mumble.

But any inspiration has long faded. I strum a few more notes, nostalgia and past glories hitting me like a freight train. My fingers freeze mid-chord, and I stare aimlessly out the windows.

Then I spot a blur of movement out in the snow, near a thick pine tree.

Is someone...*out there*?

No way. Not in this weather. It's probably just some animal.

I rise from the bed and cross to press my face against the window.

Wait.

That vibrant green hat in the middle of the snowdrift wasn't there before.

I hurriedly tug on a pair of sweatpants and a t-shirt and run to the door where I pull on my boots and coat. For a second I consider grabbing my rifle, but something tells me I don't need it. My heart pounds as I rush outside, the cold air hitting me like a slap to the face. I charge across the yard, snow crunching under me until I reach the hat.

A tiny young woman lies in the snow, struggling to sit up. There's a broken tree branch beside her.

What the fuck? Was she spying on me in the middle of this blizzard?

I pull her up into a sitting position and kneel down. "What the hell are you doing out here?"

Her pretty, green eyes go wide as they meet mine.

She doesn't answer.

"Well?" I add.

"I...um..." she stammers. "I...I'm so sorry. I didn't mean... I was..." But nothing I can work with comes out.

"We don't have all day, honey. We'll freeze our asses off out here. Are you okay to stand?"

She nods. "You're Lennox Steele," she says suddenly, almost as if in a daze.

I reach under her arms and pull her up on her feet next to me.

"Yeah. And who are you?" I ask, admiring her flaming red hair.

"I-I'm Hallie Owens," she replies almost automatically.

"Can you walk?"

She nods.

"Then let's get our butts inside. I can't feel my goddamn face," I snap, as a gust of wind cracks against my face like an icy whip. I get a good hold on her with one arm before we hurry back toward the cabin. Her steps are unsteady, and I can hear her teeth chattering.

I tighten my grip around her and hustle us inside. After removing my coat and boots, I help her out of her wet jacket.

I can't help but glance down at her heaving chest. "Sheriff's Department?" I ask, seeing the embroidered logo on the right side of her shirt. Who *is* this woman? "Go sit by the fire and grab a blanket from the sofa. Warm yourself up," I say. "Then tell me what's going on, Ms. Owens."

"Call me Hallie," she replies, heading over to the fireplace.

I notice that her gaze follows me from the room. Luckily, I keep a pot of coffee on all day. I guess I traded my alcohol addiction for one to caffeine. But I wouldn't be the first to do that, and I'll take it. I pour a couple of steaming mugs and return to the sofa, handing one to her.

Her hands are so cold, and for some reason I feel an inexplicable need to warm them with my own. But I resist the urge and instead sit next to her.

"Let's hear it, Hallie," I say, as she curls into the blanket. "What is someone from the Sheriff's Department doing out here?"

Her pale skin goes pink and she inhales deeply. "I need your autograph."

What? Did she just say autograph? You've got to be kidding me!

"You risked your life, falling from a fucking tree in the middle of a blizzard, for an *autograph*?" I grind out. I'm furious.

"Yes, but—"

"Unbelievable," I seethe, looking away to keep my anger under control. "Okay, once you get warmed up and finish your coffee, you need to leave. I should report you to the Sheriff himself. He gave me his word no one would know I was even here."

"Please don't, Mr. Steele," she pleads. "He knows nothing of this. I found out on my own. I can be pretty ingenious when I want something."

"So, stalking then?" I snap. This woman has some nerve.

"Not stalking…" she begins, and I nearly roll my eyes. "Not *completely*." She scoots herself forward and throws her shoulders back. "I swear, if you want me to leave empty-handed I will. But I had to try. The autograph's not for me, it's for my little sister, Ciara. She's your biggest fan. She has JIA—chronic arthritis—and she's had a *really* shitty year. I overheard you were in town, and I guess I hoped I could make her Christmas special with an autograph from her idol."

Shit. I didn't expect to hear that she's doing all of this for a chronically ill baby sister. My heart aches a bit. Did I also lose my sense of humanity when I lost my way with music?

"I'm sorry she's had a rough year," I say, my voice low. I rub the scruff under my chin. "Sure. I'll sign something for your sister. But then you go on your way."

If she stays here any longer, I'm positive I'll do something that'll ruin her sister's opinion of me. I wouldn't want Hallie to tell her sister what an asshole I am.

Hallie smiles. "Oh, thank you so much, Mr. Steele! Ciara's going to flip—"

I cut off her grateful words. I really don't deserve them. "Call me Lennox. Mr. Steele sounds like some vintage super-hero, and I'm anything but that."

She smiles even more brightly. I'd better get up quickly or else I might smile back. "Back in a minute."

I head to the office space just off the living room. I know exactly which album I want to sign for Ciara: *Welcome to the*

Party. It was my first and has always remained my favorite. It was pure joy to make. It also made me rich beyond my wildest dreams. But honestly, I'd give up all the money just to feel that same joy again I felt making that album. I finally find it after rifling through a stack near the window and grab a black pen.

When I return to Hallie, she's still drinking her coffee by the fire where I left her. With the glow of the flames illuminating her, she's downright sexy.

I sit next to her and uncap the pen. "How do you spell your sister's name?"

"C-i-a-r-a," she says, and I write it on the cover, together with a short note about how much I appreciate her as a diehard fan. Then I hand it to Hallie.

She beams. "She'll love it," she says, running her delicate fingers over the cover. God, I wonder what those fingers would feel like on my skin—

Watch it, Len.

"This will make her Christmas. Thank you again." She looks up, and my eyes go straight to hers.

"Even though I'm not condoning your methods, you took a risk for someone you love and I respect that. Not many people would have braved these conditions, even if it was for a very good cause." I pause for a second, thinking. "Fame has taught me that kindness from others usually comes with a price."

I'm not sure why I feel the need to tell her this. But something makes me want her to know where I'm coming from. Why I might act the way I do.

"That's too bad. I know I'd do *anything* for my family and friends. And as a proud member of the Sheriff's Department, I risk a lot for anyone…for nothing in return."

I'm in awe of her huge heart.

A gust of wind slams into the cabin, interrupting my train of thought, and we both jump, turning toward the windows.

Outside, snow is covering everything in a massive blanket of white. And it seems to be piling up at an alarming rate.

I can't let Hallie go back out in that. I need to keep her safe and sound.

With me.

"I made gumbo," I say quickly. "You might as well grab a bowl for dinner. Doesn't look like you're going anywhere for a while."

CHAPTER 3
HALLIE

I can't believe it: I'm trapped with Lennox Steele in a cabin on top of Frozen Heights.

Of all the possible outcomes of my attempt to get this grumpy rock star's autograph, this particular one never entered my mind.

After texting back and forth with Juniper, convincing her I was indeed with Lennox Steele and that I was safe, she agreed to stop worrying. I almost asked Lennox for a selfie to prove it, but I didn't want to push it.

Now, as the snow continues to blanket the world outside, cocooning us in this cozy cabin, I'm eating a bowl of surprisingly delicious gumbo that the man who once filled stadium arenas made *himself*.

"This is really good, Lennox," I say, savoring the spicy stew. "Where did you learn to make gumbo this good?"

"I have a place in New Orleans where I spend part of the year." He drags a spoon through his bowl and holds it up, watching the thick gravy drip from it. "It's all about the roux. The darker the better."

"Well, you nailed it," I say, taking another bite.

"Glad you like it," he adds, with an oddly shy smile. Then he glances into the fire. "It's...also where the rehab facility was."

Right. I heard about that, a few years back.

He clears his throat. "Anyway, I've always found cooking to be a stress reliever. And also, it's an art that's not a whole lot different from music." He shrugs. "At this point, maybe I should think of changing careers."

"Hey now," I warn, nudging his leg with my foot. "The gumbo's damn good, but your music...*loads* better."

He chuckles. "Thanks, but what good am I if I can't create new stuff anymore?" He stands quickly, as if he's done talking about it. "How about something to drink? I don't have anything with alcohol, but I can make a Shirley Temple that will blow your freaking mind."

I laugh. "Oh my god, yes. I want my mind blown."

He bites his lip, and it's so sexy. I still can't believe I'm here. After falling out of a tree in a blizzard! The world sure is crazy sometimes.

I get up too, taking our dishes. "I'll help clean up."

"You don't have to do that, Hallie," he says, pausing as he heads toward the kitchen.

God, I love how he says my name—all husky and low. "But I want to," I manage to reply, filling the huge apron sink with warm water and soap suds.

"Well, okay," he mutters, gathering ingredients from the refrigerator and pantry.

I find a container for the leftover gumbo and pack it up.

Then I hear the clinking of glasses and ice behind me. "Tell me more about Ciara," Lennox says. "It sounds like she's your top priority. Are your parents around?"

I turn around as I dry the pot I just scrubbed and rinsed. "I say baby sister, but she's sixteen years old. Our parents have done so much for her, but they're getting older so I decided to take on more of the responsibility. They deserve some time for themselves, you know? I do everything I can to make sure Ciara's happy and has everything she needs to thrive, including all the opportunities I got."

Lennox finishes making our drinks and leans against the counter, all tall and broody and sexy, his dark gray eyes taking in my every move with a mix of curiosity and something else that makes my heart flutter. "What does she love? Like, what makes her smile?"

I share stories of Ciara's love for music and animals, tell him about her shy nature and her dreams of becoming a painter despite her condition. Lennox listens intently, asking questions and offering the occasional insightful comment. He really does seem to care.

"I know it must be difficult taking on so much responsibility at your age. You're a good woman, Hallie, putting your sister's happiness above everything else. A strong one, too."

I feel a lump in my throat, the sincerity in his voice catching me off guard. "I... I do my best," I manage to say, putting away the last of the dry dishes.

He hands me my drink and our fingers brush, sending a buzz of electricity over my skin.

"I can see that. It's admirable," he continues, his gaze unwavering. "It seems like you two have a special bond. I'll bet she's incredibly proud of you."

I hope she is. My eyes well up and I silently curse myself. Why am I so emotional all of a sudden? He's just being kind. Have I really been starved for that so much? "Thank you," I say, taking a sip of my drink to distract me from any more embarrassing moments of sentimentality.

"What do you think?" he asks, nodding toward the Shirley Temple.

I take a good swig. It's perfectly sweet and fizzy. Wow. "Yep. Mind. Blown."

He grins—my god, the man has a *dimple* in his left cheek. It's barely noticeable with his scruff, but I can see it.

He's killing me.

"How about some after-dinner music?" I ask, and his smile vanishes.

"You want me to play something?"

"Of course. You're a rock star. I'd love to hear you play." I put my hands on my hips. "Unless you're going to make me wait until your next tour."

He scoffs. "If I don't write some new stuff fast, there won't *be* another tour."

"Is that why you're tucked away here in Frozen Heights? To write music?"

His toned arms fold across his broad chest, causing the tattoos to stretch. "Yeah. My manager gave me until the start of the new year to get an album done, or else he's finally moving on."

"You're okay with him giving you an ultimatum like that?" I ask, wondering if I would be able to be creative under that kind of pressure.

He smirks. "He's been extremely patient with me. I'm not good business if I'm not making music. No musician is."

"Well, I don't like him," I say firmly, irritated on Lennox's behalf.

"Not many people do," he replies with a small smile. Then he sets down his drink and walks over to grab the acoustic guitar off the dining table. "Okay, anything in particular you want to hear?"

"Surprise me." I sit on a barstool at the counter, nursing my Shirley Temple.

"Be warned, it's been a while," he says, perching on the table. "Pardon my rust, I might be a little rough."

"I like it kinda rough," I chuckle, then clap my hand over my mouth in embarrassment. I can't believe that just came out like that.

"*Okay* then..." His dark brow raises, and he laughs.

My face burns up as he begins to strum, tuning the guitar.

Finally Lennox begins to play, his fingers floating across the strings with a practiced ease and passion that belies his current creative struggles. The rich, deep notes fill the room, his tall frame bent over the instrument, dark hair falling into his eyes. The melody is hauntingly beautiful, and so raw it makes my breath catch. This isn't the music of a man who's lost his touch; it's the music of a soul baring itself, unfiltered and achingly real.

He continues to play, the lyrics speaking of love and loss, of second chances and the journey to find yourself again. I'm drawn to everything about the song, pulled in by the magnetic force of his talent and the emotion he pours into every chord.

As the last note fades away, my heart is pounding in my chest. "That was incredible," I whisper. "You have a gift. Truly, Lennox. You haven't lost *anything*."

He opens his eyes, his intense gaze holding me captive as he sets the guitar aside. "You felt it, then?"

Nodding, I whisper, "Yes. It's like...like I got to experience a piece of your soul."

Lennox smiles. "For me, it felt like I was finally breathing again after being underwater for years." His eyes flash with a spark of...passion, maybe?

His eyes fall to my mouth and stay there long enough to make me wonder if he's going to come over here and kiss me. Hell, I'm teetering on the edge of wondering whether or not I should do the same...

CHAPTER 4
LENNOX

I'm used to being the center of attention, commanding a crowd with my melodies and lyrics, sending fans into a frenzy with my every move on stage. But right now, my audience consists of one sexy redhead, and I'm not so sure I'm the master of my own destiny anymore.

The blizzard rages outside, forming an impenetrable white fortress around us. But I find myself caught in a different kind of storm—one of emotion and desire that swirls wildly within the confines of this cabin. The roaring flames in the fireplace have nothing on the ones Hallie ignites in my heart and...*elsewhere*. Every moment with her is like a sudden blast of heat in this frozen prison.

I wanted to kiss her after I had finished playing, but I didn't want her to think my feelings toward her were coming from her positive reaction to my music.

Don't get me wrong: it's nice. *Really* nice to know she gets my music. But for her to think that was the sole reason for wanting her? No. That makes me look like a shallow asshole.

And while I can be an asshole, what I'm feeling for her is anything but shallow.

She watches me tinker around on the guitar, her curious crystal-clear green eyes following my fingers.

"Come here," I say, my voice coming out rougher than I expected. "Have a seat."

I get up and have her sit on the table. I position the guitar in front of her while I get behind, so I can reach around and guide her hands.

She smells like Heaven, sweet and fresh, and being this close to her delectable neck and ear might be a mistake.

My calloused fingers entwine with hers and show her how to hold the instrument properly. Her soft skin against mine sends tendrils of awareness through my body, so unlike the numbness I've felt for years.

"Let it speak through you," I murmur, placing her hands to make the basic chords.

As I demonstrate, my fingers linger on the frets, and my voice rumbles deep in my chest as I hum a simple melody. She leans her head back to eye me from the side, her scrutiny both unnerving and arousing.

"Like this?" she asks, her voice breathless as she mimics my actions. But instead of the chord I taught her, her finger slips and a random bum note comes out that makes me wince despite myself.

"Uhh...almost," I say, and she giggles.

I guide her fingers back to the correct positions, hyper aware of every point of contact, the way her breath quickens, and the heat that sears my skin. My cock stirs to life.

"There," I whisper, my breath right in her ear. "Try again with less force."

This time the chord is flawless, and as she strums it, I lean in, playing a second melody around her. My lips ghost over her earlobe, whispering words that suddenly begin to come to me along with the tune. I feel her tremble, and my self-control begins to slip.

"I've never been very good at playing an instrument," she whispers. "But I'm beginning to learn that it's not just about the technical stuff, is it? It's about passion, right?"

"Yes. Passion and soul," I reply, my voice gravelly. "Those are the ingredients for a hit song."

She nods, then tilts her head so that her hair is tickling my face. "What was your inspiration, Lennox? What got you writing music in the first place?"

The question catches me off-guard. I stiffen, my fingers pausing on the guitar strings. "I—it was a mix of things," I hedge.

"You don't have to answer if it makes you uncomfortable," she says, clearly feeling me tense up.

What am I trying to hide? I take a deep breath. "Music is about expressing something, about tapping into what you feel and translating that into words and melodies," I confess. "For me, in the end it was about channeling my demons, my pain, and my anger. But in the beginning, I was inspired by the good times, love, and hope. It was a release."

"What about now?" she probes gently. "What's stopping you?"

I sigh, the weight of my struggles pressing down on me. "I dunno. It's like something is missing. I can't seem to tap into that place anymore…" I trail off, afraid to admit the truth.

Hallie squeezes my hand. Her gentle warmth seeps into me, offering comfort I hadn't realized I needed. "You're human, Lennox. Humans struggle. But you've got something special in you. It just needs a nudge…maybe more time."

"Time is the one thing I don't have," I say. "Deadline, remember?"

"I have faith in you," she whispers.

Doubts continue to cloud my mind, casting a pall over the glimmers of hope Hallie has ignited. What if this connection I'm feeling with her is the catalyst and inspiration I need to reclaim my former glory? Or is it all a cruel trick of the heart, a fleeting sensation born of our forced proximity?

Why can't I just have faith in myself?

I rest my cheek against her hair, inhaling her scent. Then I'm rubbing against the silky strands with my brow. My nose. My cheek.

Suddenly my lips press against the back of her neck, just under her ear.

Her entire body shudders, and her breath catches as she leans into my touch, her body sending a clear signal that I can't ignore. Don't want to ignore. I set the guitar down on the table and pull her hair away from her neck, trailing desperate kisses behind her ear.

"Are you okay with this?" I whisper, nuzzling her ear. "Because I feel like I'm standing on the edge of a cliff, about to leap into the unknown."

"How about we jump together," she breathes back.

With that I groan, softly biting at her.

She moans loudly in response and her hands find my thighs behind her, clawing frantically at them in my sweats.

"*Fuck, baby,*" I mutter against her skin. I don't want to break away from her, but I have to so I can stand and turn her around. Then I pull her back into my arms.

I capture her lips in a fierce kiss, pouring all my niggling doubts, lingering fears, and surging hope into that single moment of connection. Her lips are warm and soft beneath mine, responding with a fiery need that matches my own.

She melts into the kiss, her hands spearing through my hair, her body pressed tight against mine. Our tongues explore and dance, as the heat between us threatens to consume us both. When we finally break apart, both of us are breathless.

"I need you now, Hallie," I say, between pants.

She nods and I dip down to lift her up and over my shoulder.

Then I carry her up the stairs to my bedroom.

CHAPTER 5
HALLIE

L ennox tosses me onto the bed. "Take it all off, Red," he commands. I like the new pet name.

I mean, the man can call me anything he wants if he's going to kiss me like that.

Wow.

He quickly turns on the fireplace with the remote and kills the overhead lights in favor of some LED flameless candles placed around the room.

I sit up and pull off my polo shirt, then wriggle out of my tactical pants.

Lennox peels off his T-shirt, but when he sees me down to my bra and panties, he yells. "Wait! Stop! I want to watch this."

He sits on the bed, still in his sweatpants. "Ahem. You may continue."

I chuckle and reach back to undo the clasp. Then I slide the straps down and let the fabric fall forward.

"Oh, honey," Lennox groans. "Those are some perfect tits."

I smile, getting up on my knees so I can hook my fingers into my panties and pull them down. Then I roll back and extend my toes toward Lennox. He slides my panties the rest of the way off, his tongue nearly hanging out of his mouth.

I crawl over to him, and his rough fingertips tilt my chin up so he can give me a feather-light kiss. "You're beautiful," he whispers. I take a steadying breath as my heart races.

I rest my hands on his broad shoulders, tracing his tattoos down his chest, over his abs. "I want to suck your cock, Lennox."

"Hallie, baby," he breathes, "I wanted to lick your sweet pussy first."

"Please," I moan, pulling at his waistband.

His cock is tenting his sweats. But instead of diving right in, I lean forward and follow that spectacular, muscled "v" with my tongue.

Lennox sucks in a breath.

"I have a confession," I murmur.

"Yeah?"

"Yeah. When I was up in that tree, I may have seen you when you got out of the shower."

He chuckles, running a hand through my hair. "Naked?"

"Uh-huh. Not on purpose… I was just trying to see if you were home."

"Naughty girl," he says, in that rough, gravelly voice that makes me need to squeeze my thighs together. "Did you at least like what you saw?"

"Ohhh yes," I reply. "*Very* impressive."

"Phew," he says, laughingly wiping his forehead.

I grab hold of his waistband, pulling it out to set his long, thick cock free before I slide his sweats down.

My god, it's even more glorious up close. I run my fingers over him, loving the feel of his velvety skin and the slick contours of his shaft.

"Your touch…" He trails off, gasping when I replace my fingers with my mouth.

"*Fuck me*," he groans, as I slide my lips over the crown.

When I take him deeper, his hands tighten in my hair. "*Ohhhhh…*"

I moan along with him, sliding him in and out of my mouth, wrapping my hand around the base.

"Red, I'm so close…if you don't stop…"

I continue, redoubling my efforts, until his legs start shaking and his hips jerk erratically.

"I'm coming, baby. I'm—coming!" he yells as he climaxes hard, sending his release down my throat.

I swallow, pumping him until the very end.

"Christ, Hallie…" he says as I look up at him, my mouth sliding off his cock. "You're way too young to know how to do that so well."

I grin. "I think maybe it's like making music. All about passion and soul."

"Touché." He chuckles. "Now, spread those sexy legs and let me worship that pussy."

I shudder, his words igniting my entire body. He helps me shift up on the bed so he can crawl over me. My legs fall apart to make room for him as he leans down and kisses me—a sensual, sliding dance of tongues and eager lips.

He moves down my body, tasting every inch of my skin. He licks my nipple, and I gasp, wanting more.

"I love these tiny sensitive pink nipples," he growls, taking my other peak into his mouth and sucking, making me moan. He draws back, his teeth grazing over me, and I whimper.

He kisses down my abdomen, nipping and licking around my navel. I'm squirming, wanting his mouth everywhere, but achingly desperate for it to be on my pussy.

"Patience, my sexy little vixen," he chuckles, his hands

brushing my inner thighs, sending tingles of anticipation all through me. He gently parts my legs, and I can feel air against my most secret of places.

I glance down to see his eyes smoldering as he studies me. "You're stunning," he whispers, his voice a low rasp. "So damn beautiful and so damn ready for me."

He leans forward, his breath ghosting over my skin, and I arch toward him, biting my lip. He kisses me softly at first, his lips gentle and exploring, each feathery caress sending sparks of pleasure through me. Then, with increased purpose, he laps at my core, groaning as if he's enjoying this as much as I am. "Sweet... So fucking sweet," he moans, the vibrations from his words against my sensitive flesh sending delightful tremors through my body.

I reach down to thread my fingers through Lennox's dark hair, guiding him, silently urging him to continue. He does so with fervent dedication, his tongue lapping, stroking and swirling, exploring every inch of my pussy. He suckles and nips gently, then brushes his tongue around my clit, and I cry out, bucking against his mouth.

"That's it, baby," he murmurs against me, his breath hot on my swollen flesh. "Relax and let it happen. I want to feel you come apart on my tongue."

His hands grip my hips, holding me in place as he works me over, his skilled mouth and tongue relentless in their pursuit of my pleasure. My body tenses up, hovering on the knife edge of release, the sensations overwhelming.

"Oh god, Lennox, please," I beg, my fingers clenching his hair.

"Tell me what you need, Red. Say it," he growls.

"I need..." I stop to pant. "I need you to make me come. So fucking badly."

He presses in closer, increasing the pace. His tongue works

in firm, rhythmic motions, his scruff brushing over my sensitized skin, adding more stimulation.

I'm writhing against his face and his tongue.

It feels amazing.

"That's it, honey," he encourages, his voice rough with his own desire. "Let it all out. So sexy. Come for me, Hallie."

His words, combined with the wet, relentless stroking of his tongue, and the rasp of his stubble, push me over the edge.

I cry out, convulsing, pleasure coursing through my system like liquid fire.

Lennox doesn't let up, continuing to wreck me with his sweet torture through my climax, milking every last drop of ecstasy from my trembling body.

As my heart rate gradually slows and my breath evens out, he places soft kisses over my thighs and hips. "You are beyond incredible," I whisper, reaching down to pull him up to me.

We sink into a deep, soul-wrenching kiss.

One that I'll remember forever.

CHAPTER 6
LENNOX

"I could spend days between your legs, Hallie," I groan, pulling back to look into her beautiful green eyes. "But right now, I need to be inside you, filling you with my cock and my cum."

I'm already addicted to the sound of her moans and pleas and the amazing noises she makes as she shatters from an orgasm.

I reach over to pull open the nightstand drawer, feeling around for a condom. When I find one, I rip the foil open with my teeth as she watches intently.

She's nodding, whispering "yes" on tiny breaths.

I roll on the latex and shift my position above her, slowly guiding my length into her.

She stiffens, and I instantly pause, her wet, tight heat better than anything I've ever experienced.

"No. Don't stop. I'll breathe through it. You're just...so big," she says, her eyes squeezed shut.

"It'll be okay, baby. One inch at a time," I grit out, as I feel her thighs relax outward.

Once I'm all the way in I begin to rock, and the moan that she lets out almost undoes me right then.

"Yes…" I say, as her pussy grips me like a velvet glove. I thrust harder.

"*Lennox,*" she whines. I feel the same.

"It's so good, isn't it?"

"Amazing," she groans, her head dropping back.

I hold onto one of her thighs and focus on driving into her pussy at the exact angle where I feel her nails dig the hardest into my shoulders.

"Good like that?" I pant.

"Yes, *yes*…keep…going," she says, gasping with each thrust.

"Ahh, Hallie…." I groan, my voice ragged. "Love, I need…"

"I know," she breathes, understanding. "Just like that… I'm…"

"Do it, baby. I'm ready to explode. You feel too fucking good." I stare down at her, my hips bucking into her.

"Lennox!" she suddenly screams, as her pussy latches onto me, spasming, milking me. "I'm coming…"

"Yes, god yes!" I roar, my body convulsing as my cock erupts, pulsing, spilling my seed into her. "Goddammit, Hallie!"

She's still shaking as I ride out my climax along with her, muscles clenching and releasing like mad.

Finally, I collapse next to her, watching her sweat-glistened body heave, her fiery hair splayed around her shoulders, the aftershocks of pleasure rippling through her body.

Fuck, she's a dream.

She turns to look at me, eyes wide with wonder, something swirling in their depths that makes my insides churn.

There's definitely no going back from this.

The morning light peeks in through the kitchen window as I begin preparing the coffee. The quiet hiss of the stovetop kettle fills the silence as I scoop the grounds, my mind wandering to last night.

It's hard to find the words to describe what Hallie and I shared. We made love with an intensity that left us both breathless. I can't remember a time I've ever been so satisfied and yet left so ravenously hungry for a woman.

I remember how her lips tasted like maraschino cherries and lime from the Shirley Temples. How her skin felt like silk under my calloused fingertips. How she matched my every move with a fervor that fueled my fire. When I came inside her, her body clenching around me, it was like a tidal wave, washing away all the doubts and fears that had plagued me.

As I pour the boiling water over the grounds, the rich aroma of the coffee mingles with the lingering scent of sex on my skin, and I can't help but smile.

Just as I hear the gurgle of the coffee beginning to drip into the pot, I hear Hallie padding up softly behind me. She wraps her arms around me, pressing her face to my back. I let out a low rumble, satisfaction mixed with longing.

"Good morning, growly," she purrs, her voice laced with mischief.

"Morning, hon. Couldn't resist sneaking up on me again, huh?"

She chuckles.

"You're never going to let me live down how we met, are you?"

"Nope," I say, pouring a cup of coffee for her.

Then she slips her hands into my sweats, sliding them over my now ragingly hard cock.

I let out a strangled groan, my body already hungry for her again. It's like I'm back to being a horny teenager, experiencing this wild rush of desire for the first time.

"Mmm, just the way I like it," she says, stroking me. "Hot and thick."

"Fuck, Hallie..." I shudder, closing my eyes as she rubs over my wet tip, using my pre-cum to lube me up.

"So hard and so perfect," she whispers, teasing the ridge of my head with her sweet fingers. My breath stutters and my belly clenches as I grip the edge of the counter.

"God, baby, yeah...right there."

"Here?" she says, softly continuing her sexy torture.

"Christ, yes," I groan, my hips involuntarily thrusting into her hands. My body starts to tremble. "You're making my fucking toenails curl."

"Mmm..." She doesn't stop. "Come for me, Lennox. Right now, in my hands."

And with that she sends me over the edge, shattering the last of my control. I surrender to the pleasure, letting out a savage growl as my release explodes.

Hallie works me through my climax, my hips writhing and jerking, my cum splattering over the countertop and her hands.

I'm still panting as she moans along with me, finally letting my cock slip from her grasp.

After I catch my breath, I clean us both up quickly with a towel and then turn to pull her into my arms.

"Do you have any idea how fucking sexy you are?" I say, searching her eyes. "You drive me crazy, Hallie. Not only that, you make me question everything I thought I knew." I thread my fingers through her hair and kiss her fiercely, putting everything I have into this moment.

I'm in too deep, way over my head, but I can't bring myself to care. This woman has captivated me completely.

When I pull back, though, something in her lovely eyes has changed.

"Lennox, I need to know something."

I brace myself, expecting the worst. "What's that?"

"Are you just using me to get your mojo back, or is this real?"

Her question hits me like a punch to the gut. The truth is, I'm terrified this is all too good to be true, that my past will taint what we've started.

"It's just…" She pauses, biting her lip, a blush creeping up her cheeks. "I know how women throw themselves at rock stars. All the parties, the groupies…" She waves her hand vaguely. "I want to believe you're different, but how can I be sure?"

I exhale sharply, raking my hand through my hair. "You know I'm not a party guy anymore. The rock star lifestyle nearly killed me. And I'm not the least bit interested in reviving that part of my life." I pause, trying to find the right words to express the depth of my feelings. "Hallie, you… You make me feel alive. With you, I can be myself. It's been a long time since I felt that way."

She searches my eyes, desperately searching for truth in my gaze. "But can you promise you won't fall back into old habits?"

I step closer, wanting nothing more than to erase the uncertainty in her eyes with my touch. "I can promise you this," I begin, my voice unwavering. "I've never felt like this before. About anyone. You… You make me want to be a better man."

Hallie's breath catches, but she still looks unsure. "I want to believe you. So much. But what happens when the real world comes knocking?"

Yeah. The real world. The one that made me turn to alcohol all those years ago. Who am I kidding? Maybe I can't make ironclad promises. Nobody has a crystal ball.

I take a deep breath. "I won't deny my past, Hallie, but I don't know how else I can explain to you that I'm not that person anymore." I pull away from her, suddenly irritated "I truly don't know what else to say to you."

She lets out a shaky breath and crosses her arms over her chest. I see the battle within her. She swallows and glances down at her bare feet. "Then maybe it's just too risky for me to trust you with my heart."

It feels like a slap to the face, and I want to crumple. Instead, I head to the sink and start cleaning up the dishes.

I shrug. "In that case, maybe you should just go," I hear myself say, and it sounds so foreign—like someone else is saying it. An asshole.

She just scoffs, and then I hear her walk away. Probably up to the bedroom to get dressed.

And my heart twists painfully in my chest.

CHAPTER 7
HALLIE

I sit at my desk, my fingers nervously drumming on the wood. It's been a week since my argument with Lennox. I'm still an emotional wreck, driving Juniper up the wall with how much I talk about him—my constant outbursts, spontaneous tears, and pitiful weepy tirades. I decided not to tell my family about what happened. Ciara will still get her Christmas surprise, of course, but they don't need to know the details surrounding the night I got his autograph.

Dammit, I miss him.

The small Deepwood Mountain Sheriff's Department office is unusually quiet today. Like, where the hell is everyone? Juniper's been MIA for nearly half an hour. I haven't seen Sheriff Quinn come through for ages. Deputy Barlow hasn't popped in to ask if I needed something from the vending machine, like he always does at least once during my shift.

Even the calls have been light. All I hear is the soft buzz of the fluorescent lights above.

If someone doesn't appear soon, I'll have to jump to the only logical conclusion—zombie apocalypse.

I huff, my mind drifting to Lennox—to the snowstorm, our

intense connection, and the implosion that left my heart more broken than I would have thought possible after just one night.

I thought he understood me. But maybe I was wrong. Maybe I asked too much of him. Maybe *I'm* the one with trust issues.

Grr.

The door to the dispatch office opens and I lift my head, ready to give an earful to whichever one of my colleagues for leaving me to deal with the zombie apocalypse alone.

My heart stops as I lock gazes with the most breathtaking pair of gray eyes I've seen.

Lennox.

He stands tall and ruggedly handsome in the doorway, guitar in hand, looking like he's just stepped off the stage and into my world.

He begins to strum his guitar, and then his deep, gravelly voice fills the room, singing words that pierce straight into my heart:

In the stillness of a mountain retreat,
My muse, a fiery vision, I did meet.
When passion's flames ignited the night,
Her spirit set my heart alight.

The gentle notes he coaxes from his guitar strike a chord deep within me. A sweet yet powerful ballad.

Through shadows, she brought me to the light,
Healing this broken heart of mine.
Her love my redemption song,
Our future together, sure and strong.

My eyes fill with tears as he continues:

Like a mountain storm, you crash through my skies,
Lightning strikes, and I come alive.
Your love's the thunder in my veins,
Washing away all the pain.
Through the chaos, I've found my peace,
In your arms, my soul's release.
You're my calm after the storm,
My shelter when the wild winds roar.

I can't promise an easy ride,
But I promise I'll always try,
To be the man to make things right,
For you, forever, I'll strive.

Your love's the key to my soul,
Breaking down these walls of stone,
Together we'll rise like the tide,
In this new life, you and I.

As the final notes fade away, I'm already on my feet, overwhelmed by the raw emotion in his performance. I come around from my desk as he walks up to me, setting the guitar down by his feet.

"You wrote a song," I say, smiling into his eyes.

He smiles back. "That I did. The night we were together, after you fell asleep, I went downstairs, got the lyrics down, then added the melody. It was the fastest I've ever written something. And I've already got ideas for the rest of the album."

"It's beautiful," I reply. "Truly."

"I'd like to think that's because it's *our* song," he says, not taking his eyes off me. "I wrote that for you. For us."

I blink, stunned.

"I'm so sorry, Hallie," he says. "For years, my life was utter chaos, constant motion. I lost myself in the music, the fame that went with it. And then I had to step away and hit reset. You've brought back that joy. Made me feel alive again. Challenged me, sparked my creativity. And I realize I've been trying to fill a void, but maybe it's more about creating something new, something real.

"I don't want to go back to the person I was, Hallie. I want to create, but I also want...I don't know, a life with meaning, with genuine connection. I thought coming here would help me find my way back to music, but it's shown me something far more important."

"What's that?" I ask.

My heart pounds in my chest as he takes my hands in his. "It's shown me that I can have a future, a real future, with someone I care about. That I don't have to be that world-weary musician, lost in a bottle or chasing the next hit song. I can be more, if I let myself. And I think you can help. If you're willing."

I smile and look at our hands. "I'm sorry, too, Lennox," I say, feeling my confidence rise. "I put too much pressure on you, when I think it's my own trust issues. You got under my skin fast, and I didn't know how to handle that. I'm not used to letting anyone in, especially not someone as amazing as you. It was unfair to put any kinds of expectations on you so soon."

He shakes his head. "No, Hallie. I should've told you exactly how I was feeling and not gotten defensive. The truth is, you can trust that I'll do everything in my power to protect your heart and keep it safe. Because that matters to me." He takes a deep breath. "I love you, Hallie."

My entire body takes flight at his words. I reach up and

take his sexy, stubbled face in my hands. "And I love you, Lennox."

He pulls me closer and leans down to capture my lips. This kiss is unlike any we've shared before. It carries all the weight of the storms we've weathered, the barriers we've broken, and the love we've found.

Soon, there's a chorus of cheers, whistles, and applause, and we break apart to see my colleagues at the door.

Juniper winks at me—the little sneak!

I rest my head on Lennox's chest and chuckle softly.

Only a kiss like that could make me forget an oncoming zombie apocalypse.

EPILOGUE - LENNOX
FOUR MONTHS LATER

I stand backstage at my first concert in Montana since the release of my new album, breathing deeply, trying to focus. My single "Mountain Storm" has been sitting at the top of the charts for weeks and I couldn't be more thrilled. The last few months have been a whirlwind of rehearsals, media interviews, and fan meetups. Now, as the familiar buzz of the crowd reaches my ears, reminding me of the countless times I've been in this very position, the nerves I feel are...different. This performance is deeply personal; not only is it my official comeback, but also, more importantly, it's a tribute to Hallie—to us.

It's been several months since the blizzard that changed my life, and I can't believe how far I've come. That isolated cabin now feels like a distant memory, a turning point in my journey of self-discovery. And here I am, on stage, ready to share my hit song—*our* song—with the crowd.

As the band backing me begins to play a vamped intro, I take a deep breath, steeling myself for the surge of emotions I know will hit once I step into the spotlight. The shadows of my troubled past still lurk around the edges of my mind, but I find it easier to push them away these days. And that's all down to the incredible woman who brought me back to life.

I walk onstage, casting a long shadow under the bright lights. The crowd erupts in cheers, their energy warming my heart. I grin, feeling a sense of comfort and familiarity as I take my place behind the mic.

"Welcome, everyone," I address the audience, my voice steady. "For those of you who have been waiting patiently, wondering if I'd ever return to the stage, I'm happy to say that your patience has been rewarded. Tonight, I'm not just here to sing for you. I'm here to celebrate new beginnings, rebirths, and the power of love that can mend even the most broken of hearts."

A chorus of cheers and whistles fills the arena, and I let out a low chuckle, feeling that unique connection that I've missed, the one between a performer and his audience.

The opening chords from Jake on the piano start, a haunting melody that sets the tone. I close my eyes, taking a moment to ground myself as the spotlight bathes me in warmth.

"This next song is very special to me," I continue, picking up my acoustic guitar from the nearby stand. "It's a song about finding light in the darkness, about discovering that some- times miracles happen when you least expect them. I was lost, struggling to find my way back to the world, until an angel as bright as the stars burst into my life."

The crowd is still cheering and whistling like crazy as I turn briefly to look offstage. When I see Hallie standing there in the wings next to her sister Ciara, I wink. "Hallie—my savior, my muse, my love. I wouldn't be where I am today without you. This song's dedicated to you, baby."

She smiles at me, and I begin to sing.

When I finish, I feel like I've poured every single drop of my soul out onto the stage.

The audience goes wild, leaping to their feet.

"Thank you," I say quietly, looking out to the crowd. "Thank you very much."

Once the arena settles down, I ask. "What do you say: you guys want to meet her? Hallie?"

The crowd cheers loudly, and I walk over to the side of the stage and take her hand, pulling her gently onto the stage, much to the delight of the audience.

"'Mountain Storm' isn't just about me," I say, as I look deeply into her eyes. "It's about us. Hallie and I met during a massive snowstorm. After five years of creative silence, she coaxed music back into my life. But more importantly, she started bringing love and sunshine into my life every single day. So, I'm making it official."

I get down on my knee and pull the ring from my pocket. "Hallie, will you be mine...forever?"

The audience erupts into even louder cheers and applause, and Hallie's eyes fly wide. She laughs, covering her mouth. She nods and stammers out a yes, and I slide the ring on her finger before I stand and she jumps into my arms. We kiss deeply, as the crowd nearly brings the house down.

When we finally pull apart, I look off to the side to see Ciara giving me a huge smile and a big thumbs up. I told her two weeks ago that I would be proposing tonight, making her promise not to tell Hallie. She was thrilled to be entrusted with the secret. I know that I have gained not only the love of my life, but also the love of her family. And that is something no amount of fame can ever come close to touching.

I turn back to Hallie and she smiles at me, her eyes wet with happy tears.

I can't wait to spend the rest of my life making beautiful music with this woman.

CAPTURED BY THE
BRAWNY VETERAN

CHAPTER 1
RO

The snow crunches under my boots like it's got a personal grudge against them, each step a battle versus the frozen, unforgiving terrain. I huff out a breath, watch it transform into a cloud of mist in the frosty air, and mutter a choice word or two about my brother's impeccable timing.

Max—*the genius*—double-booked us, and now I'm trudging up to a remote cabin in Frozen Heights as the daylight dims, hoping to squeeze in this cleaning job before the storm hits.

The cabin looms ahead, rustic and weather-beaten, nestled among towering pines and covered in a blanket of snow. It's picturesque enough, I suppose, if you're into the whole secluded, woodsy vibe. The snow-capped peaks of Deepwood Mountain are admittedly a winter wonderland. But me? I'd rather be sipping hot cocoa in my centrally heated apartment right now, thank you very much.

Smoke curls lazily from the chimney, so at least I know I won't be cleaning an icebox. I make it to the front porch and stomp the snow off my boots at the doorstep. When I knock, the door creaks open under my fist.

Who leaves their door unlocked out here?

Frowning, I poke my head inside. "Hi there! I'm here from Ever-Green Cleaning."

No answer.

I take a tentative step forward, my eyes sweeping over the sparsely furnished space.

"Hello? Anyone home?" I call out.

Still nothing.

This is actually perfect. I always get done much faster without anyone in my way. I shrug off my coat and hang it on the rack by the door, then put my various cleaning supplies in the kitchen, ready to get to work.

The cabin is small, just a living room, kitchen, bedroom, and bathroom. Weirdly, it's already almost spotless, and tidy in a way I recognize immediately.

Military.

Max learned how to clean when he was in the Marines. After he got out he decided to start a business and thought a cleaning service would be something he'd be good at. I joined the company right after I finished high school. We've been successful, even if there are occasional hiccups—like *cough* double-booking—every once in a while. But I'm super proud of him.

Proud of *us*.

The place is in good enough shape that I'll only have to do a quick refresh—counters, floors, a bit of dusting. As I work, I play my usual game of noticing little details to get an idea of who lives here. Definitely a reader, judging by the stack of dog-eared books on the coffee table. Camo and tactical gear hang on the walls, and travel mementos laid out neatly on a desk hint at a well-traveled person.

Plus, they've got impeccable taste in coffee, if the gourmet beans next to the coffeemaker are any indication.

Everything's already organized in the pantry and the refrigerator.

Wow. There's not much to do here at all.

I head to the bedroom, my eyes immediately going to the vast king-sized bed. The sheets are plaid flannel, look soft, and they smell like pine and soap.

A man's scent for sure—and a rugged one at that.

I decide the bedclothes probably need washing, so I begin stripping them off the mattress.

A floorboard creaks behind me, and suddenly I'm being yanked backward, strong arms lifting me clear off the ground. I cry out before I'm slammed onto the bed. The air whooshes out of my lungs and I've barely had time to register the cold blade against my neck when a deep, gravelly voice growls, "Gotcha, Goldilocks. Now tell me who the hell you are and what the hell you're doing in my house."

I freeze, my heart hammering right up into my throat. I'm pinned down by the man's considerable weight, and I can feel the bulky muscles of his chest pressed against my back and a rigid arm locked around my waist. But it's his voice that really gets me—low, commanding, and laced with a threat that sends a shiver down my spine.

"I'm the maid," I manage to squeak. "I was sent to clean your cabin."

"ID. Now."

I gesture to my back pocket. "In my wallet."

He keeps one hand on my shoulder, as his other one slips into the pocket of my yoga pants. There's rustling and a slap of leather.

"Aurora Green. 25. Deepwood address. And look-e here, a couple of business cards for Ever-Green Cleaning with your name on them." He reads in a husky whisper that makes my insides squirm.

"Well, I guess you're legit." Slowly, the steel against my neck is removed, and the pressure on my back eases. I scramble to turn over and am finally able to take in the man looming over me.

He's huge, towering even when kneeling on the bed. His hair is sandy blond, streaked with gray and cropped short. My gaze wanders over his chiseled face and thick, salt-and-pepper beard. Wow... This guy has seen some things. His eyes are a piercing amber, like a wolf's, and equally intense. They scan me, and a flicker of confusion crosses his stern face.

"You didn't have to tackle me like a linebacker, you know," I snap, finally recovering my breath.

"You're lucky I didn't do any worse," he grunts, crossing his beefy arms. "I didn't schedule a cleaning."

"You didn't?"

He gestures around broadly. "Does this place *look* like it needs cleaning?"

Hmm. He has a point. But what if he's not...you know... completely with it? I mean, he *did* just jump me with a knife. "This is 105 Snowpeak Place, right?"

"Wrong. *150* Snowpeak Place," he says, sheathing the knife.

Oh god... I'm at the wrong cabin! *Shit.* Did I fuck this up, or did Max? I huff out a long breath. "I'm so sorry, Mr.—"

"Wagner. But everyone calls me Duke."

I push myself up onto my elbows, uncomfortably aware I'm still lying on this man's bed. "Duke, I—"

"I was out back chopping some wood. Did you not think to check the perimeter of the cabin before entering?" He relaxes his stance slightly, but his amber eyes are still locked onto mine, analyzing, judging.

Sarcasm bubbles up, my typical defense mechanism kicking in. "Normally, yes, I do a thorough sweep of the entire property, checking for potential hazards like rabid squirrels, moose in heat, and angry grizzly bears with knives. But it was getting late." I roll my eyes.

My joke falls flat, the lines around his eyes creasing as he scowls.

"Although I *did* wonder what kind of fool would leave their door unlocked up here," I add, just to be petty.

His frown deepens. "I was only a couple of yards away."

I hold his gaze, unwavering. Man, he's got sexy eyes.

Finally, he blinks. "You should be more careful. Armed cabin owners may not hesitate to fire at a trespasser."

That sounds like something Max would say. "Well, you are the first to hold me at knifepoint," I reply with a small smile, rubbing my throat, my pulse finally slowing.

He doesn't smile back, but his eyes soften when they drop to my neck. Then he extends a hand to help me up.

I take it, feeling the calluses on his large, warm palm as he pulls me to my feet. "I go by Ro," I offer, noticing how his meaty hand dwarfs mine.

He nods, stepping back to give me some space. The way his eyes rove over my body brings a rush of heat to my face.

"Ro..." he murmurs, like he's testing the name on his tongue. "Sorry about the...misunderstanding. Old habits die hard."

I raise an eyebrow. "Old habits?"

He runs a hand through his hair almost self-consciously.

"Army. Twenty-five years. You don't exactly leave that behind so easily."

I knew it! The military-style organization, the rigid neatness. And the slight overreaction to finding a stranger in his house—even if it was a woman stripping off his sheets in order to launder them.

All jokes aside, I can't imagine what he's seen or been through.

"Just got out this year," he adds.

"My brother who runs our family cleaning business is a former Marine. He had a bit of a tough time transitioning back to civilian life at first, too."

Duke nods, his eyes avoiding me. It's obvious he doesn't want to talk about it further.

"Let me just put your sheets back on, and then I'll be out of your hair."

"Don't worry about the sheets," he says, touching my arm to stop me. It sends an electric current zipping through my whole system. He pulls back quickly, as if he might have felt something too.

Hey, a girl can hope, right?

There's something about this brooding bear that intrigues me, making me wat to know the story behind those intense eyes. I'll bet it's something rough and wild and—

"You should go," he says brusquely.

Okay, then.

I go to gather my things when the cabin door suddenly bursts open, smacking loudly against the wall, and an arctic blast sweeps into the room.

"Holy shit!" I clutch at my chest, heart racing as we see the deep snow that's piled up outside.

Duke grudgingly stomps over and shoves the door closed, locking it and making sure it's secure.

"I take it back: you're not going anywhere, Goldilocks."

CHAPTER 2
DUKE

I'd been out chopping wood, the rhythmic thud of the axe biting into the grain echoing through the crisp air, each strike a controlled burst of pent-up energy.

Splitting logs has always been more than just a chore for me; it's a meditative ritual, a way to keep my hands busy and my mind quiet.

But as I was making my way back to the cabin, a slight movement behind the window caught my eye, a flicker of a shadow that shouldn't have been there. My years of training in the service kicked in and I instantly snapped into combat mode, sneaking over to the front door and slipping inside.

Then I tackled the intruder in my bedroom before I could stop to think who it might be.

I'm not a civilian. I'm a soldier: always prepared, always vigilant, always waiting for the next battle.

More to the point, I hadn't been expecting anyone—especially not a sunny little blonde with dazzling hazel eyes and curves a man could happily sink into...forever.

Ro bristles, her chin lifting defiantly. "You can't keep me here against my will."

I sigh, dragging a hand through my beard. "But it's not safe. The storm's already here. I guarantee you wouldn't even make it back to your car, let alone down the mountain."

Her chest heaves as she sighs and looks out the window, drawing my attention to her full, round breasts, the outline of her stiff nipples under her shirt scrambling my brain.

She bites her lip, brow furrowing. "But...I can't stay *here*. My brother is going to flip out—"

"Call him," I say firmly. "What choice have you got? You're snowed in. If he has any sense...and since he's a military man, I'm sure he does...he'll understand."

"You don't exactly have a guest room," she mutters darkly.

"You can sleep on the couch. It's closest to the fire." I shrug. "It's not much, but it's better than freezing to death in a blizzard."

She sighs, resignation settling into her pretty eyes. "Well... fine. Thank you for this, I guess."

I nod, satisfied that at least she's seeing reason now. The cabin suddenly feels smaller, warmer, and I'm acutely aware of her presence, her intoxicating scent—sweet, flowery, fresh and overwhelmingly feminine.

It's...very distracting.

I shake my head. I'm not here for distractions, dammit. I came to Frozen Heights for solitude, for peace and quiet, so I could work on myself. *Alone.* Not be cooped up with an achingly curvy blonde who smells like springtime.

Ro pulls out her phone and I step into the bedroom to give her some privacy.

The sound of her voice, animated and warm, filters through the wall as she speaks to her brother. I need to get out of these wet clothes, but more than that, I need a moment to breathe and collect my thoughts.

The fabric of my shirt clings to my skin as I peel it off, the chill from the snow still lingering on my body. I tug on a long-sleeved thermal and a pair of worn sweatpants, the comfortable clothes a stark contrast to the discomfort I feel inside. The woman in the other room has invaded my mind—her smile, her spirit, her curves—and made this old grizzly weak.

Ro is far too sunny and vivacious for someone like me. I'm battered and broken, more at home in the cold darkness than in her warm light. Plus, I'm in my forties, and she's only... what did her license say...25? Good god. A lifetime of experience and baggage separates us.

But even as I think about all this, I'm automatically pulling out a set of warm, dry clothes for her. The thought of her being cold—of her needing *anything*—gnaws at me. I want to take care of her, provide for her, even if it's just something as simple as a warm sweater and a pair of comfy sweatpants.

When I step back into the living room, her hazel eyes look up at me, traveling over my body. There's something hungry in her gaze that makes my cock stand up and take notice.

I must be imagining it. There's no way in hell this vibrant, young woman could want someone as weathered and scarred as me.

She swallows before speaking. "Max isn't exactly thrilled." She sets her phone down on the coffee table. "But he understands there's not much we can do, not with this storm." She pauses. "However, he *did* want me to mention he's totally Googling you."

I nod, appreciating her brother's protectiveness. "As he well should."

She gives me a small smile and I rush to speak, eager to change the subject. "I put out some clothes for you on the dresser, if you're interested." I rub the back of my neck. "They'll be way too big, but at least they're warm and dry."

She smiles again and it hits me right in the chest. "Thanks, Duke."

I grunt in response, uncomfortable with her gratitude. I'm just being practical. Survival 101—feed her, keep her warm, keep her alive. Basic logistics, that's all.

She disappears into the bedroom and I turn to the kitchen, gathering ingredients for our dinner. It's almost like we're a normal couple, snowed in and making the best of it, not the much-too-young ray of sunshine and the grumpy old bear that we really are.

When she walks back into the kitchen, I stifle a groan. Her silky blonde hair is down, falling in soft waves over her shoulders. Her curves fill out my sweater and sweatpants like a wet dream, straining against the fabric in a ways that makes my mouth go dry. Thank god I'm standing behind the counter so she can't see how turned on I am.

"Hungry?" I ask, my voice coming out gruffer than I intended.

She looks surprised. "A little," she admits, and there's a flush staining her cheeks that wasn't there before.

"Let's fix that," I reply, wishing she'd let me satisfy that hunger in other ways.

CHAPTER 3
RO

"You cook?" I ask, watching as Duke organizes the ingredients in front of him.

"The military taught me self-sufficiency," he says, rolling up his sleeves to reveal corded forearms. "Cooking's a survival skill."

I nod. "Max taught me to cook when I was a kid," I say softly. "After our parents died, I mean. We had to learn to do a lot of things on our own."

His gaze shifts toward me. I didn't mean to blurt that out, but for some reason I want to connect with this guy on a deeper level.

"I'm sorry," he whispers, empathy in his eyes that tells me he's seen loss, too. "How old were you?"

My eyes brim with unshed tears. "Sixteen," I reply, my voice a little shaky. "Max was twenty-eight. He left the Marines to take care of me."

"He sounds like an honorable man," Duke says with a small smile. Something passes between us. An understanding that we're both fighters, both survivors. In different ways, though: where I've chosen light and laughter to fight the darkness of my past, he seems to still be figuring out which way he wants to go.

"He is," I admit, watching Duke prowl around the kitchen like a grumpy bear who's just woken up from hibernation. Damn. He's got that whole rugged, mountain man thing going on, and despite him being so damn prickly, I'm swooning like a heroine in a romance novel.

You're being ridiculous.

I try to lighten the mood, throwing out some jokes, but he's gone back to being about as responsive as a stone wall. His contrasting moods—gruff and distant one moment, surprisingly tender the next—are really frustrating.

"You know, I'm more than willing to help cook," I offer as he moves back and forth preparing our food. "I'm seriously starting to think you're worried I'd set the place on fire, though."

He pauses, casting a glance over his shoulder that's somewhere between annoyed and amused. "I'm just not used to... people," he grumbles, running a hand through his hair. I suddenly find myself wondering what those locks might feel like under my fingers.

I raise an eyebrow. "People in general? Or just cheerful ones?"

He grunts, turning away, and I smile inwardly. There's something about his gruff exterior that makes me want to chip away at it, like an ice sculptor revealing the masterpiece hidden within.

I can tell he's used to being in charge and doing things himself. But there's a tension in his shoulders and a stiffness in his movements that makes me wonder if he's not *quite* as okay as he at first seems.

As he cooks, the cabin fills with the warm, inviting scent of tomatoes and spices. I watch as Duke expertly chops vegetables, his hands steady and sure, and let myself imagine what it would be like to be touched by those hands—*really* touched.

Down, girl.

I shake the thought from my head, focusing instead on the food. "That smells amazing," I say, my stomach rumbling in agreement.

Duke looks over at me, a hint of a smile on his lips. "It's just pasta," he shrugs. "Nothing fancy."

"Well, it *smells* fancy," I reply, grinning. "And I'm not exactly picky."

"You're the perfect guest, then," he says, and I chuckle.

We eat in a silence that is surprisingly comfortable while sitting on the floor, setting our plates on the coffee table. The only sounds are the crackling of the fire and the howling of the wind outside. The pasta is truly delicious, and I find myself eagerly devouring every bite, much to Duke's apparent amusement whenever I catch him stealing glances at me.

"Tell me more about your brother," he says suddenly.

I shrug, trying to keep my voice light. "I love working with him, but he can tend to be a little...overprotective. Sometimes it's nice, but other times, it makes me feel that he doesn't trust me to take care of myself."

Duke is quiet for a moment, turning back to the fire. "He just wants to keep you safe."

"I know," I counter gently. "But at times, it feels like he's holding me back."

Duke looks at me curiously, his eyes reflecting the dance of the flames. "Really? From what?"

I hesitate, biting my lip. It's not something I talk about often, but there's something about Duke and the quiet strength he radiates that makes me want to open up.

"From...the world," I admit softly. "From exploring.

Living. From meeting new people…" I take a deep breath. "Sometimes, I think he's afraid to do all that himself, too."

Duke gazes at me, then turns back to the fire, the silence settling between us again, and I wonder if I've said too much.

Is he holding himself back from living, same as Max?

I try my luck at finding out more about him. "So, how about you?" I ask. "Do you have any family?"

Duke tenses up, his grip on his fork tightening. For a moment, I think he's not going to answer, but finally he speaks, his voice low. "A younger brother," he says. "And a nephew. They both live in Bozeman."

"That's nice," I say. "It must be great having them so close."

He nods. There's clearly more to the story, but I don't push.

Duke's expression darkens. "It is," he says after a moment, his voice tight. "It's also…complicated."

I wait for him to elaborate, but he doesn't. Instead he stands up, clearing the dishes with abrupt, jerky movements. This time I can tell I've upset him, though I'm not sure exactly how.

I stand up too, gently taking the plates from his hands. "Hey," I say, my voice soft. "I've got this. You cooked, it's only fair I clean up."

Duke's eyes meet mine for the first time in what feels like a while. The raw vulnerability I see in them makes my heart ache. But then he blinks, and the moment is gone, his expression shuttering once more.

He steps back. "Okay. Thanks. I'll stoke the fire."

I watch as he throws in another log, poking at it with the iron rod. This man is a frustrating, fascinating puzzle that I'm suddenly desperate to solve. But for now I turn my attention to the dishes, letting the warm sudsy water soothe my nerves.

What is it about this grump that draws me in? Is it the way he carries himself, with quiet strength and confidence? Or the way his eyes seem to want to pick me apart and find all my secrets, just as much as I do his?

Maybe it's just that he's *insanely* hot.

I shake my head, laughing at myself for being so silly. This is just a temporary situation, a mere blip in the grand scheme of things. Once the storm clears, I'll be on my way, and Duke will be nothing more than a distant memory…

And that makes me a little sad.

With a sigh, I finish the dishes, drying my hands on a nearby towel. When I turn to leave the kitchen I nearly run smack dab into Duke, who's standing in the doorway, his massive frame taking up most of the space.

I let out a yelp of surprise. "Jesus, you scared me," I say.

Duke doesn't move, the intensity of his gaze locked on mine making my breath hitch.

"Sorry," he says, voice hoarse. He doesn't sound sorry at all. He sounds…hungry.

I swallow hard, trying to find my voice. "It's okay," I whisper, my heart slamming in my rib cage. "I just…didn't see you there."

Duke takes a step closer. I can feel heat radiating off his body and see the rise and fall of his chest with each breath. I want to reach out and touch him, to run my hands over his broad shoulders and feel the rough texture of his beard against my skin.

Instead I stand still, frozen in place by the sheer force of his amber gaze. And then, slowly—so slowly it's almost painful—he reaches out and grasps a wisp of hair near my face.

He slides his fingertips down, brushing my cheek. It's barely more than a whisper of skin on skin. But it's enough to send a surge of electricity coursing through me.

We just stand there as desire pools in my core, our breath mingling in the space between us. And then, with a soft,

LEXI HAYES

almost imperceptible sigh, Duke steps back, and the spell is broken.

I blink, feeling dazed and disoriented. What the hell just happened? Was that real?

Or did I imagine the whole thing?

CHAPTER 4
DUKE

My control is slipping.

This woman makes me want things I haven't wanted in a long time, and I'm not sure how much longer I can be around her before I snap.

I nearly kissed her in the kitchen just now, for god's sake!

All I know is, if she keeps looking at me like that, with a desire that seems to match my own... Wild horses couldn't stop me.

Ro is straightening up around the cabin, her curves swaying gently, her smile as bright and cheery as the morning sun. She's humming a tune, something light and sweet, a huge contrast to the storm raging both outside and within me.

I shouldn't be looking at her this way. It's wrong.

People like me don't get sweet little rays of sunshine falling in love with them. But the storm, my isolation, the way she lights up this cold, lonely cabin—it's playing tricks on my mind. Making me want things I have zero business wanting.

She turns to me, her hazel-green eyes sparkling. "Duke, have you thought about what you want to do now that you're a civilian?"

The question catches me off guard. I've been so focused on just getting through each day avoiding the things I know I *don't* want—noise, chaos, reminders of the past—that I haven't really considered what comes next. "Dunno," I admit gruffly. "Haven't given it much thought."

She tilts her head, allowing her golden curls to swirl around her shoulders. "Really? You must have some ideas. What about your dreams? Your passions? Things you always wanted to do but couldn't because you were busy in the military?"

I lean back on the couch, thinking. Dreams? Yeah, I guess I had those before the military took over my life and became my entire identity. Before I saw things that can't be unseen and turned me into a man who seeks solitude over society.

"I used to want to build things," I say slowly, the memory surfacing like an ancient artifact. "Houses, maybe. Something tangible that would outlast me."

Ro's face lights up, her smile wide and encouraging. "So do it! There's always a need for good builders around here."

Her optimism is sweet. But I've seen and done too much to be a dreamer anymore. I stand up abruptly, wanting to put some distance between us. "It's just an old idea. Nothing more."

She pouts slightly, her lower lip jutting out in a way that makes me want to bite it. "Well, I think it's a *great* idea. And I think you should go for it. I mean, what have you got to lose?"

I turn away from her and face the storm raging outside the window. The wind howls, and the snow swirls relentlessly. It's a harsh, unforgiving sight, but it's familiar. Comfortable. It doesn't make me want things I can't have.

"Duke?" Ro's voice is soft, and much closer than I expect. I turn to find her standing right next to me, her hazel eyes filled with concern. "You okay?"

No, I'm not okay. I'm drawn to you in a way that scares me.

She curls her fingers in the fabric of my shirt and leans in closer, her luscious lips inches away, her pulse fluttering at the base of her throat. Desire surges through me, hot and intense. I want to kiss her. Claim her. Lose myself in her sweet body.

"Careful, Goldilocks," I warn, my voice hoarse with restraint.

She doesn't move, just runs her tongue over her lip, leaving a sheen of moisture that begs to be licked away. I fight the urge, every muscle in my body tense with the effort.

When her eyes drop to my mouth, I lose the battle.

I pull her up to meet my lips, crushing her to me. I kiss her deeply and frantically, my hands tangling in her hair. She melts against me on a moan, arms wrapping around me, fingers digging into my shoulders. It's rough and desperate, two people clinging to each other in a fiery explosion of need.

We stumble to the couch and I lower her onto the cushions, never breaking the kiss. Her body is so soft beneath mine, her luscious curves fitting perfectly against me. My hands explore like they are starving for her, tracing the dip of her waist and the flare of her hips.

"Duke," she gasps, arching into my touch, shuddering.

I trail kisses down her neck, my hands sliding under her sweater, needing to feel her skin, so warm and smooth beneath my fingers.

When I brush the edge of her bra, reality suddenly crashes down on me. I'm moving far too fast, taking advantage of her and the situation. She's young, innocent, and *way* too good for me.

I pull away abruptly, breathing heavily. "Sorry, Ro. I lost control. It's been a long time."

She looks up at me, her eyes glazed over with desire, her lips swollen from our kiss. "It's okay, Duke. I want it too."

I shake my head and stand. "It's *not* okay. We can't... We shouldn't get carried away."

Hurt flares in her eyes. "Why? You regret it?"

I do. I don't. I'm torn between wanting her and knowing I'll just hold her back...like her brother.

But I wait too long to answer, and she's moving away from me.

"Let's just go to bed," she says, her voice monotone. She tugs the blanket around her like a shield.

That's my cue to exit.

I walk to my bedroom, pausing at the door.

Part of me wants to rush to her, pull her into my arms, and never let go. The other part remembers the scars on my soul.

What can I possibly say? That I'm afraid if I let her in, she'll see the monster inside me?

I can't drag her into that.

And so I just close the door as the storm rages outside, same as the war within me.

CHAPTER 5
RO

I toss and turn on the couch, the blankets twisted around my legs. But if my body is restless, my thoughts are even more so. The brawny, brooding veteran in the next room who seems to be made of equal parts granite and thunder clouds is driving me *crazy*.

One moment he's looking at me like I'm the sunrise after a long, dark night. The next he's pulling back, retreating into his cave like a grumpy grizzly bear.

That kiss…*god*, that kiss. It was a match struck in the darkness, a sudden flare of light and heat that promised to turn into a wildfire, if only we had let it burn.

But then he doused the flame, leaving me breathless and utterly confused.

I see the way he looks at me, the naked desire that pools in his amber eyes. So why the hot and cold routine? Is he scared? Does he think I can't handle him?

I mean, *please*.

I sigh, punching the pillow into a more comfortable shape. I'm not a naive little girl. I know what I want, and I'm not afraid to go after it. And right now, I want Duke, with his growly commands and his unexpected smiles that make my heart flutter and my panties soaked.

The fire in the grate might be down to embers, but my body is burning up, humming with need.

You know what? If Duke's too stubborn to admit what he wants, maybe I need to give him a little push.

I sit up and am tearing the blankets off me when a strange moan suddenly echoes through the cabin, stopping me.

It comes again—low, pained. My mind immediately goes to the stories Max has told me about veterans and their nightmares. I tiptoe quietly to Duke's bedroom, worried he's having some horrible PTSD episode.

I raise my hand to knock, but another moan stops me. This one is different, deeper, and...oh. *Oh.*

A shiver runs through me as I realize what's happening on the other side of the door. That's no nightmare. *That's—*

Before I can talk myself out of it, I push the door open.

The sight that greets me nearly brings me to my knees.

Bathed in the warm glow of a nightlight, Duke is sprawled on the bed, the sheets tangled around his tree-trunk thighs. His sculpted muscles are taut as a big hand strokes his thick, hard cock. With his eyes closed and head thrown back, the sound he's making isn't one of pain or fear.

It's raw, uninhibited pleasure.

I should leave. I should turn around, walk away, and give him his privacy in his own darned home. But I'm rooted to the spot, my eyes glued to the intoxicating sight of him in ecstasy. He's magnificently sexy.

My body responds instantly, wet heat pooling between my thighs. Every inch of him is chiseled, from his broad shoulders to his washboard abs. A thin trail of hair leads down from his navel to the base of his shaft. I want to trace it with my tongue. I want to be the one touching him right now, driving him wild.

He moans again, this time even more deeply and gutturally, his hips lifting off the bed, his hand moving faster.

I squeeze my thighs together, trying to ease the ache building inside me. And suddenly, a small, needy sound escapes my own throat.

His eyes snap open, his hand freezing mid-stroke. "Ro?" He stares at me, shock and embarrassment warring in his expression. He pulls the sheet up to cover himself. "I—"

"I heard you, and—" I take a step closer, my heart pounding in my chest. "I'm sorry, I thought you were having a nightmare."

He groans and shakes his head. "This isn't... I wasn't..."

"Were you thinking about me?" I ask, keeping my voice steady despite the butterflies in my stomach.

He pushes up onto his elbows, his brow furrowed. "What?"

"When you were...touching yourself," I say, taking another step closer to the bed. "Were you thinking about me?"

He hesitates, then swallows hard, making his Adam's apple bob. "Yes," he finally admits, his voice hoarse. "Goldilocks, you're the sexiest woman I've ever seen."

A thrill runs through me. The thought of this strong hunk of a man getting himself off to *me* is intoxicating and empowering.

"But you shouldn't be here," he continues. "I'm... I'm no good for you."

I take another step closer, until I'm standing right beside the bed. I look down at him, at the worry etched into every line of his rugged face. "Really?" I ask, my voice soft. "Or are you just scared?"

I reach out, trailing my fingers lightly over his bare chest, and his muscles tense beneath my touch.

He captures my hand, his fingers wrapping around my

wrist. "I'm not the man you think I am," he growls. "I've done things I'm not proud of. Seen things I can't forget. It's broken me. You deserve so much more."

I kneel down and reach my other hand out to stroke his cheek, his beard rough against my palm.

"Why don't you let me be the judge of that?" I say, dragging my fingers down his chest and over the ridges of his abs. He gasps, his body responding to my every caress.

"Ro..." he rasps. "What are you doing?"

I meet his eyes. "Touching you," I say quietly. "I want to chase away those shadows in your eyes. Make you forget everything for a while."

His pupils dilate. "You don't have to," he says roughly.

"But I want to...so badly."

His eyes search my face. "How did I get so lucky?" he asks, as I trace over the sharp V-lines of his hips.

"Fate and a wrong address?" I say with a smile.

He huffs out a laugh. But when I wrap my hand around his cock it turns into a long groan, his hips lifting off the bed again. He's hot and hard in my hand, his skin like velvet stretched over steel.

"You're huge," I murmur, my thumb brushing over his tip.

He shudders, a drop of slick fluid coating my fingers.

"May I take you in my mouth...make you come?"

"Goddammit, Ro," he moans. "You're going to kill me if you keep talking like that."

I grin. "So, that's a yes?"

"It's a *fuck*, yes," he rasps, watching me lean down and press a soft kiss to the head of his cock. He hisses, his hands fisting the sheets as I swirl my tongue around him, tasting his skin. He's so big, so deliciously thick...

My lips slowly slide down his veined shaft, inch by inch,

until he hits the back of my throat. He groans even louder, hips trembling as I suck him deeper.

I look up at him, my eyes meeting his as I swallow the head, the muscles of my throat working around him.

He lets out a string of curses, one of his hands tangling in my hair.

"This feels so fucking good," he whispers.

I start to bob my head up and down slowly, my hand working in tandem with my mouth.

He's shaking, his body tense and coiled like a spring.

God, I want to make him come undone.

He watches me with hungry eyes, his jaw clenched—raw need in his expression that matches my own. I love the way he fills my mouth, the way he tastes, the way he responds to my touch. He deserves to feel good...get some relief from the demons that haunt him.

I pull back, my lips sliding off his cock with a soft pop. "You like seeing me on my knees, sucking your dick?"

He groans, his hips jerking. "Hell yes," he says, his voice rough. "You're so fucking sexy, Ro. You're my good girl, aren't you?"

That phrase sends a wave of white-hot pleasure shooting through my body. I moan around him, quickening my pace. His hand tightens in my hair, his hips trying to match my rhythm.

"I'm close...so fucking close," he hisses through gritted teeth.

I slide off him quickly. "Come for me, Duke. Let me taste you."

I suck hard on the swollen tip and his hips jerk forward. He roars, and I feel his cock pulsing in my mouth as his seed spills down my throat. His release is hot and salty on my tongue and I swallow it eagerly, taking every last drop.

When he's finally spent, I pull back and smile up at him, his body glistening with sweat.

"Fuck...me..." he says between heavy pants. "That was goddamn amazing."

He reaches for me and I crawl up into his arms. He kisses me, his tongue sliding against mine. It's dirty and hot, and I love it. Our hearts pound in unison, his body still trembling from the aftershocks of his climax.

I snuggle into him. "I'm not scared of you, Duke," I whisper. "I'm not afraid of your past, or your demons, or whatever it is you think makes you unworthy of love. I see the man you are...and I am *not* running away."

He squeezes me tight and presses a kiss to my head. "I swear, you're some sort of angel," he rasps. "*My* angel."

I smile into his chest, his body warm and solid against mine. This is where I belong. Where I want to be. If I have to prove to this grizzly bear that he deserves love, I will.

One touch, one kiss, one step at a time.

CHAPTER 6
DUKE

The world gradually comes back into focus as I lie back, panting like I've just run a marathon through enemy territory.

But this isn't a battle. This is something else entirely. It's the ultimate surrender.

I've tasted this hurricane of a woman's lips, felt her touch, and had her exquisitely wicked mouth on my cock. She's unleashed the beast, and now I need more.

I need *all of her*.

I flip her onto her back, pinning her wrists above her head. Her breath catches. "Your turn to get devoured, Goldilocks," I growl. I push her sweater up and lift her briefly to pull it over her head.

I groan at the sight of her large, round tits, nipples stiff, just waiting to be sucked.

I kiss along her neck, her collarbone, her sternum—each touch of my lips eliciting a gasp or a moan. Then I lavish attention on her breasts, taking my time, teasing the sensitive peaks with my lips, tongue, and beard until she's writhing wildly beneath me.

Moving lower, I rip off her sweats and claim every inch of her skin as my own with a possessive kiss.

When I reach her wet pussy, I look up at her. Her eyes are hooded and her lips are parted. So sexy. "You're a fucking dream," I tell her, my voice low and fierce.

Then I dive in.

She tastes like heaven: sin and salvation rolled together. I feast on her, using my tongue, my lips, my teeth—every weapon in my arsenal to bring her pleasure. Her moans are music to my ears, her hips bucking against me as I nudge her closer and closer to the edge.

"Duke," she whines. "I'm… I'm going to…"

I don't stop. I don't even slow down. I tease and taste her until she's coming all over my face, her body convulsing with her release.

I don't give her time to recover.

I can't. I need her too fucking much.

I climb up her body, positioning myself at her entrance. I pause, giving her every chance to tell me to stop, but she doesn't. Instead, she pulls me closer, wrapping her sweet thighs around my waist, urging me on.

"You feel so good," I groan as I slide into her. She's tight, wet, and beyond perfect. Her nails dig into my back and her heels press into my ass, pulling me deeper.

I start to move, slowly at first, then faster and harder. I can't get enough. Her scent, her touch, her taste—I'm already addicted. She meets me thrust for thrust, her body moving in perfect sync with mine.

This intense connection is unlike anything I've ever experienced. All I want to do is chase this high.

"You're *mine*," I growl, the words tumbling from my lips before I can stop them. "Mine to touch, mine to taste, and mine to *fuck*."

She moans in response. "Yes," she yells. "Yours. Only yours."

That's all I need to hear. I lose any last shred of self-control, pounding into her with everything I have. The sound of our bodies slapping together fills the room with a primal symphony that drowns out everything else.

She feels so good. So right. Like she was made for me and me alone. Even as I think that, a part of me is still rebelling. I'm a goddamn mess, a man with too much blood on his hands and too many ghosts in his past.

But I can't stop now. Not when she's so close to the edge again. When I'm moments from sailing over it with her.

"Come with me," I command huskily. "Come with me, Ro."

She does. Her back arches as she cries out my name, her body convulsing around me. I'm right there with her, my body wracked with pleasure as I explode into her, filling her again.

I roll off her, pulling her into my arms. And then we just lie there for a long time, our bodies entwined.

"Ro, there's something I need to tell you," I finally say.

She looks up at me, eyes shining with warmth and understanding. "You can tell me anything, Duke," she says softly. "You know that."

So—I do. I tell her about the mission that changed everything, the one that pushed me to finally leave the military. I tell her about the lives lost, the blood on my hands, the guilt that still eats me up alive. I tell her about the darkness, the loneliness, the struggle to find my footing in this new life as a civilian.

She listens, her expression never wavering. And when I'm done, when I've spilled my guts and laid my soul bare, she smiles—a soft, sweet smile that lights up her face and warms the cold places inside me.

"Thank you for telling me all that," she murmurs, her fingers brushing against my cheek. "I'm guessing it wasn't easy."

"No, it wasn't," I admit, and let out a long sigh. "But with you, it feels...safe."

She grins, her eyes shimmering. "You *are* safe with me, Duke. And you always will be."

That's the moment. That's when I know, without a shadow of a doubt, that I'm in love with this woman. This spirited little spitfire who barged into my life and turned it completely upside down.

I know it won't last, though. I have too much baggage. I can't drag her into my world, into my darkness. She deserves better than that, more than what I can give her.

As we drift off to sleep, I make a decision. It's going to kill me, but come morning I'll take her back to town and let her go, for her own good.

Even if it will feel like I'm saying goodbye to a piece of my soul.

CHAPTER 7
RO

I wake to a gentle nudge, my eyes fluttering open to see Duke's stern face mere inches from mine. He moves back and I see he's already dressed in his sexy, rugged best—flannel, jeans, and combat boots.

There's a coldness in his eyes that wasn't there last night, though.

"Wake up," he grumbles. "Time to go."

I blink away the sleep, trying to process his words. "Go... where?"

"Home," he says, his voice as rough as sandpaper. "Storm's over. Best you leave now."

I sit up, pulling up the sheets to cover my bare breasts. The cabin is cold, but that could honestly be from Duke's icy expression. He's retreating, pulling back into his shell. I can see it in the determined set of his jaw, the distant look in his eyes.

"You're kicking me out?" I ask, unbelieving.

After the amazing night we had? The nerve!

He doesn't answer, just focuses on some distant point outside the window.

I stand, wrapping the sheet around me. "Fine," I say, stomping toward the bathroom. "Let me just get dressed."

I slam the door shut behind me, the sound echoing through the small cabin. I lean against the sink, looking at my reflection in the mirror. My eyes are bright, but my cheeks are suddenly flushed with anger and hurt. I splash cold water on my face, steeling myself for the confrontation I know is ahead.

When I re-emerge in my clothes, Duke is waiting by the front door. His gaze runs over me, lingering for a moment before he looks away. I can see the struggle in his eyes.

"I know what this is about," I say, stepping closer. "You're running. You're afraid of what's happening between us, so you're running away."

His jaw clenches, a muscle ticking in his cheek. "I'm not *running*," he insists. His tone lacks conviction. "I'm just… You deserve better than an old, broken-down soldier with more scars than sense."

I scoff, rolling my eyes. "Better?" I echo. "Better is *boring*, Duke. Better is safe and predictable. Better doesn't make my heart race and my skin tingle, or make me feel alive."

He looks at me, his amber eyes tortured. "You don't understand," he counters. "I'm not whole, Ro. I'm not…*right*. I can't be what you need. I can't give you the light, the happiness—"

"Stop right there," I interrupt, poking a finger into his chest. "I think you're just afraid. Scared of feeling, of living. Scared of loving."

He captures my hand, holding it against his chest. I can feel his heart pounding wildly. "You're right," he admits, his voice hoarse. "I'm terrified. What if I let you in and then you realize I'm not worth it? What happens when you see the monster inside me and run away?"

I soften my gaze, cupping his cheek with my hand. "What happens when you realize I'm not going anywhere?"

I whisper. "I don't believe in monsters, and I'm not afraid of the dark. I'm not some fragile flower that needs to be coddled."

He leans into my touch, his eyes searching mine. "You say that now… But I couldn't stand the idea of being the one who dimmed your light."

I shake my head, my heart aching. "You won't dim anything," I assure him. "You can't. Because I won't let you. I know what I want, Duke. I know *who* I want. I'm not naive. I know there are risks. Life is short, and messy, and yes, scary. But what we have here… I think it's worth the risk."

His eyes search mine, their amber depths unsure. "You're asking me to trust in you."

"No," I say, firmly but gently. "I'm asking you to trust in *us*. To take a chance on something real and true. Something that could be completely amazing."

He closes his eyes and squeezes my hand. He's almost trembling, teetering on the edge between fear and hope. And I'm right there with him, my heart in my throat, my future in his hands.

"I… I don't know if I can," he admits. "I don't know if I'm strong enough."

I smile, my thumb brushing against his cheek. "Please— you're the strongest man I know. You've faced down enemies, survived wars, served your country. You've taken so many huge risks. Now I'm asking you to take the biggest one of all, with your heart."

His eyes begin to shimmer. "You make it sound so simple." There's a hint of a smile tugging at his lips.

"It *is* simple," I say, smiling back. "It's just love, Duke. Messy, complicated, beautiful love."

He takes a deep breath, his body shuddering when he exhales. Then, finally, he nods. "Okay," he says, his voice filled with determination. "I'll try. For you, Ro, I will try. Because I love you."

"And I love you too," I reply, my heart swelling.

I lean up on my tiptoes and press my lips to his, sealing our shared promise with a kiss—a kiss filled with longing, with passion, pointing to a future that's brighter than any I'd dared to dream.

I know that no matter what comes next or whatever challenges we face, no matter what storms we weather—we'll take them on together.

And really, that's all that matters.

EPILOGUE - DUKE
SIX MONTHS LATER

The fire dances in the hearth, casting a warm glow over Ro's beautiful naked body.

She's lying back on the fluffy rug she bought to put in front of the fireplace, her wrists bound lightly above her head. Her eyes sparkle with anticipation and maybe a little nervousness, but she's a fearless one, my Goldilocks.

Her eager breaths make her luscious breasts heave tantalizingly in front of me. I grin at the sight of her, a sense of savage satisfaction washing over me. This is a battlefield I'm learning to navigate—a dance of give and take, of power and surrender.

I straddle her, my knees planted firmly on either side of her hips. Her hazel eyes follow me as I reach for the feather duster. I'd originally bought it as a joke, a playful nod to her job as a maid, but seeing her lying there, helpless and trusting, has my cock throbbing and my mind spinning with darker ideas.

"What exactly are you planning to do with that?" she asks. I can hear the slight quiver in her voice, the desire. It has my own body thrumming with excitement, too.

I lean down, ghosting my lips over hers. "I'm going to make you scream, Ro," I murmur, my voice low and gruff.

"Then I'm going to make you beg for mercy. And *then*, I'm going to make you come so hard you see stars."

Her eyes widen, pupils dilating. I feel the heat radiating off her dewy skin. She's completely turned on, her body primed and ready for whatever I have in store.

I sit back and run the soft feathers over her skin, starting at her collarbone and trailing down to her breasts. She shivers, her nipples stiffening into peaks. I circle them with the fronds, teasing her with them before leaning down and capturing one tight bud in my mouth.

She moans, her back arching off the floor as I suck and nip at her sensitive flesh. I lavish attention on one breast, then the other, all the while trailing the feather duster over her stomach, her thighs, her pussy.

She squirms beneath me, her hips thrusting up in a silent, desperate plea for more.

"Not yet, Goldilocks," I murmur against her skin. "Papa Bear wants to play first."

I sit up, holding the feather duster like a weapon. I start at her feet, running the feathers over her soles, up her calves, over her knees. She giggles at first, the sensation ticklish and light. As I move higher, the giggles turn to gasps, her body tensing with anticipation.

"How about here?" I ask, trailing the duster over her inner thighs. She writhes, trying to clamp her legs shut, but I easily hold them apart with my free hand. I lean down, my breath hot on her skin. "Maybe…here?" I ask, sliding the feathers over her pussy lips.

She chokes out a cry, her body convulsing with pleasure at the playful torture. I can see wetness glistening on her mound, smell the musky scent of her arousal. I want to bury my face in her folds, to taste her sweetness on my tongue. But not quite yet.

Not until she's begging for it.

I move the duster up to her stomach, trailing it over her sensitive skin. She squeals and bucks underneath me, her body trying to escape the ticklish sensations. I hold her down and continue to tease her in all her secret places.

"Duke, please," she gasps, breathless. "I can't take anymore."

I chuckle roughly. "You can and you will," I growl. "You'll take whatever I give you."

I move the duster up to her breasts, trailing the feathers over her nipples again. She whines, back arching, her body wriggling beneath mine. She's getting wetter and wetter.

I dip my fingers into her folds, rubbing her clit in slow, torturous circles, just how she likes.

"Duke, *please*," she moans, her voice an aching cry. "I need your cock inside me."

I smile, a victorious grin that stretches across my face. *This is what I wanted*—this desperate need. I want her to crave me like she craves air, to need me like she needs water. I want to be her everything...

I toss the feather duster aside, my hands going straight to her hips. I flip her over, keeping her hips raised in the air. Her pussy glistens with wetness as I trace a path from her clit to her luscious ass with my tongue.

"Ohhh!" she cries.

"You taste so fucking good, Ro," I growl, voice raw. "I swear, I could eat you all day."

I slide my fingers into her pussy, fucking her hard and fast. She moans and bucks against me, chasing her release. I can feel her pussy clamping tighter, her muscles clenching around my fingers. I know she's close, her orgasm building like a raging wildfire.

Fucking hell, I'm so hard.

I pull my fingers out, my dripping cock poised at her entrance, and slam into her to the hilt. My hips thrust in a frenzied rhythm as I climb higher and higher.

"I'm going to come, Duke!" she screams, her body convulsing around me, her inner walls milking my cock.

My own orgasm sits right on the edge, the pressure building in my balls.

"Do it, my love. Let me rub that sweet little clit to help you." I reach around, my fingers finding her bundle of nerves and moving in firm, fast circles as I continue to pound into her.

"God, *yessss!*" she finally cries out, as her orgasm crashes over her.

I follow, roaring to the heavens, my cock pulsing, my seed bursting into her with hot, forceful spurts.

We collapse onto the rug, our bodies slick with sweat, our breath coming in ragged gasps. I pull her against me, my arms wrapping around her, holding her close. I can feel her heart racing in her chest and the aftershocks of her orgasm rippling through her body.

I nuzzle her neck, my lips pressing a line of soft kisses along her skin. "You're mine, Ro," I murmur.

She turns in my arms, looping her bound wrists around my neck. "You bet I am, soldier," she whispers, her face flushed. "I love you so much, Duke."

This is what I've been searching for—this connection, this love. It's what makes life worth living.

I hold her close, feeling our hearts beating in time with each other. I'll never let her go, never stop fighting for her—for us. And I'll spend the rest of my life loving and cherishing her, making her happy.

After we catch our breath, I untie her hands and scoop her into my arms. "I have something to show you."

She smiles a soft, sweet smile that lights up her face and

my entire world. "Okay, shoot," she says, her expression curious.

I carry her to the window where we can see my workshed in the back yard. I've left my latest piece of furniture in front of it, one I've poured my heart and soul into, one I've crafted with love and devotion and skill.

It's a wedding arch, made of cypress.

Ro's eyes go wide, her hand covering her mouth.

"Duke," she whispers. "It's beautiful. It's...perfect."

I set her on her feet and smile, a slow, satisfied grin that fills my heart and soul. "I'm glad you like it," I say, beaming with pride.

She turns and looks up at me, her eyes filled with happy tears. "Does this mean...?"

I nod, my heart pounding. "Yes. Marry me, Ro," I say, taking her hand in mine. "I want to spend forever with you, making you happy."

She smiles, tears slipping down her cheeks. "Of course I'll marry you," she says. "I'll always be happy, as long as I have you."

And with those words, we kiss again, to forever and always.

～

RESCUED BY THE RUGGED PRINCE

CHAPTER 1
JJ

The snow whips around me, stirring up a maelstrom of icy, dancing flakes. I squint against the onslaught, my eyes tearing up from the cold.

Great. Now my eyelashes will freeze.

I've only been on this trail for an hour, and I'm already in danger of becoming a human icicle.

Gee, Penny, thanks for suggesting this little adventure smack dab in the middle of storm season. *She* found her happily ever after in this very same winter wonderhell, and naturally thought a dash of Frozen Heights magic would cure my own chronic singledom.

Riiight.

I can just imagine her now, cozied up with her hunky mountain man Mitch, sipping hot cocoa by the fire, watching some *Avengers* movie for the millionth time. Meanwhile I'm out here becoming Jack Frost's bae.

Don't get me wrong. I'm super happy for my BFF. She deserves all the joy in the world. But I can't help but be a little wistful. I mean, Mitch *worships* her.

And me...I've never even been on a date, let alone had someone look at me the way he does at her.

But I'd agreed to her idea, told her I *wanted* to come here—be one with nature and all that. Find some cute animals, some majestic beauty, and some much-needed solace in the icy wilderness.

"You'll love it, JJ," she said, her eyes all starry, her voice shining with newlywed bliss. "The fresh air, the breathtaking views, the sense of accomplishment—it'll be good for you."

I swear, sometimes I have no idea what happened to her. *I'm* the one who reads fluffy romances and fairy tales, you know?

Regardless, the only thing I'm accomplishing right now is a stunning impression of a bitter snow cone.

I sigh, trying to spot the elk that led me off the beaten path earlier, my boots sinking further with each step. Finally, I catch sight of my supposed guide again, charging ahead, almost mocking my slow progress. "Laugh it up, Bambi," I mutter under my breath. "How well would you fare if your antlers froze over?"

My words are lost to the wind. I hug my coat tighter around me, grateful for the thermal layers but cursing myself for not packing a pair of snowshoes. Or a sled. Or a team of huskies to pull me out of this frozen nightmare.

My teeth are chattering so hard I'm afraid I'll chip a tooth. If I die out here, lord help me, I'll haunt Penny so she'll never have a moment's peace.

I can almost hear her laughter as she shakes her head, telling me to stop being so dramatic.

Too damn bad. I get dramatic when I'm panicking.

I spot a small shed—or what I sincerely *hope* is a shed—in the distance. With renewed determination I push forward, my legs burning from the effort. The elk bounds ahead, disappearing into the whiteout. I stumble after it, my breath coming in ragged puffs.

Come on, I urge myself. Heroines in romance novels always find a way out of these kinds of predicaments. Usually right into the arms of a handsome stranger…

I snort. Ha! If there's a handsome stranger out here, he's probably a yeti. Or maybe a werewolf. *Girl gets lost in the woods, meets sexy, supernatural beast-man, and they live happily ever after in his cozy cave.* Isn't that how it goes?

Maybe in books. In real life, girl gets lost in the woods and ends up a cautionary tale on the evening news.

The shed is closer now, but the wind is picking up, howling furiously. I'm leaning forward into it, every step a battle against the elements. It's like nature is saying, "No happy ending for you, babe."

I finally reach the shed, pounding on the door with a fist that feels like it'll shatter into a thousand frozen shards any second. "Hello?" I call out. "Is anyone around? Please—I need help!"

Silence.

I bang again, my strength waning. This is it. I'm about to become an ice sculpture for no one's amusement but the local wildlife.

I try the handle, but it's locked. Of course.

"Anyone? Please?!" I yell in desperation.

My legs are threatening to give out from cold and exertion, and I slump against the shed. My vision is starting to blur, the edges going fuzzy. I blink rapidly, trying to clear it, but it's no use. The cold is seeping into my bones, numbing my limbs, and making my thoughts sluggish.

I close my eyes just for a second, and suddenly—

I'm not in the snow anymore. I'm in a meadow, the sun shining down, warm on my skin. There's a picnic blanket spread out, loaded with all my favorite food. And sitting across from me is...*a yeti*? Really?!

I open my eyes wide when the yeti morphs into a man. A *very* handsome man, tall and broad-shouldered, with blond hair and eyes as blue as a summer sky. He smiles at me, and I feel warmth spread deep in my belly.

"Hi," he says, his voice a low rumble that sets my heart fluttering. "It's okay. You're safe now, JJ."

I reach out to touch him, but my hand goes right through him, like he's made of mist.

And then he's gone, and I'm back in the snow, shivering and very much alone.

Sooo... Now I'm *hallucinating?* My mind is trying to conjure up a hero to save me? That's...sad.

I take a deep breath, trying to muster the strength to keep fighting. But the cold is winning, dragging me down into nothingness. I slide down the door and tumble to the side, my limbs heavy and unresponsive.

I lie there for a moment, staring up at the swirling snow. It's almost hypnotic, the way it frolics and twirls. Pretty. I feel my eyelids growing heavy, the cold seeping into my core.

No, no, no! I shake my head. Do *not* fall asleep out here. You are going to get up, and you are going to find shelter.

But even as I think that, I know I'm in trouble. I try to push myself up, but my arms give out, and I collapse back into the snow.

"This is it," I whisper, a sense of resignation washing over me. "This is how I die."

Frozen to death in Frozen Heights.

Irony at its best.

Everything suddenly feels distant, like a dream. My consciousness begins to fade away...

And then, just as everything goes black, I hear footsteps crunching in the snow. A hand touches my shoulder, and a deep, soothing voice says, "I've got you, miss."

And even as I cling to that voice, I'm swallowed by the darkness.

CHAPTER 2
VALRIC

The wind is a relentless beast today, howling through the trees like Garm, the wolf who guards the gates of Hel in Nordic myth.

Which out here happens to be a *frozen* hell, mind you.

I'm gathering firewood, my hands numb despite the thick gloves, eager to return to the warmth of my cabin when I hear it—a faint cry for help. I pause, listening intently, wondering if my mind is playing tricks on me. But then it comes again: a desperate plea, weak and barely audible.

I drop the firewood and set off toward the sound, my heart pounding. The voice is faint, but it's unmistakably feminine, and every protective instinct in me roars to life.

At the door to a small shed near the edge of my property, there's a crumpled figure in the snow.

"I'm coming!" I call out, quickening my pace. I rush to her side, crouching down to check her pulse. It's there, but alarmingly weak. Her skin is like ice, and her lips are tinged blue. I need to get her warm, fast.

"I've got you, miss," I murmur. She stirs slightly at the sound of my voice, but her eyes remain closed.

Carefully, I lift her into my arms. She's light, her body fitting perfectly against mine. Her scent, even masked by the snow and wind, is sweet and alluring. I shake off those thoughts, focusing instead on getting her back to the cabin.

She's mumbling—some nonsense about yetis and Penny owing her hot chocolate. She's clearly delirious, but I find her ramblings charming.

The trek is slow, the snow deep. But I push on, driven by a deep need to protect this woman. When I kick open the cabin door, a welcoming warmth hits us. I lay her down gently on the sofa in front of the fireplace, then stoke the flames until they roar back to life.

I gently brush the damp hair from her face. She's pretty: the contrast of her pale skin against her raven-black hair is stunning. It also leaves me eager to see what color those eyes are.

But first I need to check for any signs of injury. I strip off her wet gloves, boots and socks, inspecting her hands and feet before rubbing them briskly to bring back some warmth. Her clothes are soaked so I remove those too, grabbing a pair of sweatpants and a thermal shirt from my dresser and putting them on her. I work quickly, averting my eyes for her privacy as best I can.

I've never...uh...seen a naked woman in the flesh. So to speak.

She seems physically unharmed, just cold. I grab a thick woolen blanket from the chest near the fire and drape it over her, tucking it gently around her shoulders. As I do, she stirs, her eyes fluttering open.

For a moment, she looks at me with a dazed, dreamy expression.

Hazel. Her eyes are a beautiful hazel.

"Who are you?" she demands, her voice rough but filled with fire. "And where am I?" Her gaze sharpens and she pushes herself up against the armrest, poised as if debating to run or to fight.

"I'm Valric. You can call me Val. You're in my cabin. I found you outside, half-frozen."

She eyes me warily, then glances around the room. "In Frozen Heights? Are you some kind of mountain man? A yeti in disguise?"

I chuckle, running a hand through my overgrown beard. "Do I really need to shave that badly?"

She pulls the blanket tighter around herself. "Um...no. I... uh..." She stutters. "When you're freezing to death, I guess your brain comes up with all sorts of crazy stuff." She looks at me, her eyes narrowing slightly. "You look familiar. Do I know you from somewhere?"

I hesitate, wondering how much to reveal. My instinct is to tell her the truth, but there's something refreshing about the fact that she's treating me like any other man.

"I don't think so," I say, my tone light. "I'd definitely remember you if we'd met before."

She blinks, worrying her lower lip. It's back to a healthy pink color and watching her do that tugs at my groin. She studies me, her expression guarded. "What are you doing up here, anyway? You a park ranger? Hermit?" Her hands clench the blanket. "Serial killer?"

I raise an eyebrow, amused. But I don't want her to fear me. Might as well come clean. "None of the above. I'm a prince, here to escape the pressures of royal life."

She snorts. It's both derisive and endearing. "Right. And I'm Queen of the North Pole."

Her disbelief is a novelty and makes me grin. Most women swoon at the mere mention of my royal lineage, but not this one. "I assure you, I am. Prince Valric of Thornfjord, at your service. My family's kingdom is a small region nestled between Sweden, Norway, and Finland."

She rolls her eyes. "Okay, Prince Charming. Whatever you say. I'm JJ Young. A regular citizen. Zero royal pedigree." She huffs. "Now, where's my phone?" She looks down at her clothes, a sudden realization spreading over her face. "Did you change my clothes?"

I nod, my face heating. "They were soaked, Miss Young. I had to get you into something dry."

Her cheeks go pink.

"I swear I did so swiftly without looking at anything..."

"Oh god." She runs her hands over her face.

"For too long," I add with a playful wink, and stand to grab her phone.

I hand it to her and she hesitantly takes it, her eyes darting to mine and then away.

She taps at the screen, then lets out a frustrated sigh. "I sent a text to my friend Penny, but it doesn't seem to have gone through."

"Reception has been spotty because of the storm," I say, making my way over to the kitchen. "Apologies."

"Just great. Stuck in a cabin with a delusional prince wannabe."

I chuckle, filling a kettle with water and setting it on the stove. "Rest assured you are safe here. Once the storm clears, I'll help you get back to wherever you need to be."

She looks up from her phone. "Why should I trust you? You could be anyone."

I lean forward over the kitchen island and dip my chin slightly. "Because, Miss Young, I give you my word. And a prince's word is his bond."

She scoffs, but there's a hint of a smile on her lips. "Fine,

Prince Valric. But if you turn out to be a yeti in disguise, or secretly a mass murderer, I'm going to be *super* pissed."

I laugh. This woman is like no one I've ever met. And her doubt only has me wanting to prove I'm worthy of her trust.

"Let's just focus on getting you warm and rested, miss," I offer. "Tea or coffee? Unfortunately, I don't have any hot cocoa —which I heard you mumbling about earlier when I brought you in."

Her face goes pink again, and I find I'm enjoying making her blush. "Tea, please. And you can call me JJ."

At least she trusts me enough to let me use her first name. That's a start.

"So… What brings you to Frozen Heights?" I ask, leaning against the counter after I switch on the kettle. "It's not exactly the most hospitable place this time of year."

She shrugs, a wry smile playing on her lips. "My friend thought it would make for a nice hike. She knows I'm an animal lover and enjoy being out in nature. Also, she found her happily ever after in these mountains. I think she figured I might, too."

Interesting. "And?"

She chuckles, a sound that's a mix of bitterness and sad amusement. "Obviously, I got closer to finding frostbite and a painful death. But the scenery was nice…and I did see an elk. Though he was the reason I left the main trail. I shouldn't have followed him. What an idiot."

"A buck?"

She nods.

"They're beautiful," I reply, as the kettle begins to whistle. "I'm an animal lover, too. And I'm glad he led you astray. I might not have met you otherwise." I drop a tea bag into a mug and pour boiling water over it before handing it to her.

She takes the mug. When her fingers brush against mine

there's a spark, a warmth that has nothing to do with the tea. She looks up at me, hazel eyes searching mine. "Yeah," she says softly. "I'm kinda glad, too."

There's a moment of charged silence between us, a pause filled with possibility. Then she clears her throat and I start to make myself my own cup of tea. "So…mountain man, what's your story? Why are you hiding out up here?"

"Who says I'm hiding out?" I sit down on the edge of the couch, a small smile on my lips.

She shakes her head. "Nope. No way. People don't come to Frozen Heights unless they're trying to get away from something." I fight a shiver when I watch her delicate mouth blow on the steaming tea. "If you're not a yeti or a serial killer, what are you? A fugitive? A secret agent? A mad scientist conducting illicit experiments in the woods?"

I laugh, genuinely amused by her theories. "Nothing so exciting, I'm afraid. I told you: I just needed a break. Royal life can be…complicated."

Her expression softens slightly. "*Any* kind of life has a way of being complicated sometimes."

I nod. For whatever reason, I feel a strange connection between us. "It does. But sometimes those complications lead us to places…and people…we never expected."

She smirks. "Are you saying I'm not what you expected? Okay, what *do* you see when you look at me?"

I let my gaze travel over her, maybe a little too boldly. "Strength. Bravery. Independence." I cock my head to the side. "I see someone who is guarded but caring, who uses humor to mask her vulnerabilities. I also see someone who is beautiful, not just on the outside but in her spirit, in her fire."

She blinks, clearly taken aback by my words. She opens her mouth to say something, then abruptly snaps it shut again. Then she laughs, a sound that's half amused, half self-deprecating. "You're pretty good, you know. You almost have me believing your prince charming story."

I smile. I understand her refusing to take me at my word. I'm a complete stranger.

She's sipping her tea, her eyes thoughtful as her guard slowly lowers. She's a breath of fresh air in my otherwise stifling life.

I watch this skeptical Snow White who's upended my world and I make a silent vow.

I will keep her safe.

I will win her trust.

She may not believe in fairy tales, but I'm determined to make her believe in me—not the prince, but the man.

Although that, I think, is perhaps going to be the biggest challenge of all.

CHAPTER 3
JJ

"Hungry?" the supposed Prince Valric—or *Val*, as he insists I call him—asks. He does have a slight accent that makes me think that he should be doing an Ikea commercial. But that doesn't mean he's royal. Just, like, not from Montana.

My stomach rumbles. I guess fighting for your life in the cold really makes you work up an appetite.

"I could make us some soup?" he offers. "Nothing fancy, but it'll warm you up."

"Sure, thanks. I guess I am kinda hungry."

He's standing by the fireplace, poking at the logs with an iron rod, his profile illuminated by the flames.

Damn, he's...*really* hot. Even hotter than the fire he's stoking. He's got that whole rugged outdoorsy thing going on, with shaggy blond hair and a beard that's just the right side of scruffy. Together with his thick muscles and disarming blue eyes, I'd swear he could be a hero in one of my romance novels.

But this is not a romance novel. It's real life. And in real life, princes don't go around rescuing damsels in distress and cooking them soup. They have servants to do that—well, at least the soup part. And they certainly don't look like they belong on the cover of a mountain man calendar.

Let's review: I'm in an unfamiliar cabin, wearing a stranger's clothes, with a guy who claims to be royalty. Yeah, because that's not sketchy at all.

I glance down at the gray sweatpants and black thermal shirt he dressed me in. I still can't believe he did that. He even removed my underwear!

My cheeks heat…*in addition to other body parts.*

"You're staring," he says with a playful smirk.

I blink, coming back to my senses. "I'm just trying to figure out if I hit my head harder than I thought. There's no way any of this is real."

He chuckles, deep and warm. It does funny things to my insides. "Why is it so hard to believe? A kind stranger rescues you from a storm, nurses you back to health—"

"Changes my clothes," I interject, raising an eyebrow significantly.

He has the decency to look slightly embarrassed. "Only because it was necessary. They were soaking wet from the snow."

"Well, Val, while I appreciate the gesture, it's still a bit creepy."

He busies himself in the kitchen. "Fair enough. I apologize if I made you uncomfortable. That wasn't remotely my intention."

I wave him off, trying to act nonchalant. At least he's being decent about it all. "It's…fine. I'm just not used to being in strange cabins with strange men who claim to be royalty."

He grins, and my stomach does a little flip. How does someone get a jaw so chiseled? "Well, I'm not used to rescuing beautiful, sarcastic women from blizzards, so I guess we're even."

Um… That's the second time he's called me beautiful. I shake off the compliment, focusing on the more pressing matter. "You're really sticking to your prince story, huh? If you really are a prince, you're not very princely. I mean, you're cooking soup in a rustic cabin. Isn't that what your staff is for?"

"Ah, but up here, I'm just Val. No titles, no expectations, no staff. Just a man enjoying the simple life."

He walks over and hands me a steaming bowl, our fingers brushing briefly. There's that spark again, a jolt of electricity that I'm chalking up to static or some other scientific phenomenon. There's no way I'm feeling anything for this guy. Nope.

"Careful," he warns, winking and sitting down next to me on the couch. "It's hot."

Yeah, it sure is. And I'm *not* talking about the soup.

I take a spoonful and blow on it to cool it down a little before trying it, and when I taste it my tongue dances with delight. Damn it, why does he have to be a good cook too?

"This is really delicious," I say.

"I'm glad you like it," he replies, eating a few spoonfuls himself. He reaches into the pocket of his track pants and pulls out his phone.

"How about I show you where I'm from?" he says, tapping a folder on his phone screen and pushing it over to me on the couch. "It's really beautiful."

I pick it up and start scrolling through photos of an admittedly, yes, *stunning* landscape: snow-capped mountains, vast forests, a grand castle nestled in the heart of it all. It really is like something out of a fairy tale.

"Thornfjord," he says quietly. "My home."

I bite my lip and push the phone back to him. "Okay, so you've got some pretty pictures. That doesn't prove you're a prince."

He laughs. "What can I say to convince you?"

I shrug, taking another spoonful of soup. "I don't know. Tell me something *princely*. Something only a true royal would know."

He thinks for a moment, then leans forward, his eyes crinkling at the sides. "In Thornfjord, it's tradition for the royal family to have a private sauna in their quarters."

I snort. "A sauna? *That's* your big royal secret?"

He grins. "It's not just any sauna. It's fed by the waters of a hidden spring that runs underneath part of the castle. Legend says it has healing properties."

I roll my eyes, hiding a smile. "Magical healing saunas. Right. I suppose you have a pet unicorn, too?"

"No unicorns, sorry. Just a lot of reindeer."

I chuckle, finishing my soup. "I do love reindeer."

"Then you'll have to come and visit," he says.

Despite my skepticism, I'm finding it harder and harder to resist this guy's...charm. If that's what this is. He's got this ease about him, a gentle playfulness that's endearing.

But I'm not the kind of girl who falls for charming princes or magical saunas. I'm a realist, even if my reading preferences lean toward the romantic. And the *reality* is, I'm stuck in a cabin with a stranger who could be *anyone*.

I set the empty soup bowl on the coffee table. "It's just weird to me that you're out here roughing it in the wilderness, cooking soup like a regular Joe. Don't you have an entourage? Bodyguards and all that jazz? Heck, where's your crown?"

He laughs. "We don't usually wear the crowns around the house. Only on special State occasions." He leans back against the sofa. "And I told you already: I came here to escape all that. To just be Val, not Prince Valric."

I huff, crossing my arms. "Okay, say I believe you. Say you really *are* a prince. Why would you want to escape the luxury, power, and your adoring subjects? I'm sure the…what did you call them, complications…aren't *that* bad."

His smile fades, a shadow passing over his stupidly handsome features. "Sometimes, the weight of expectation can be too much. The constant scrutiny, the lack of privacy, the pressure to be perfect—it's suffocating."

I raise an eyebrow and give him a nudge. "Hmm… Sounds to me like you need a better PR team, not a cabin in the woods."

He chuckles, his dark mood lifting. "Perhaps. But for now, *right here* is where I want to be."

I have to admit, I'm beginning to buy into his story. "You have more photos? You know, of your family and stuff?"

The edge of his mouth quirks up as he scrolls through his phone again and lays it in front of me.

I take it and feel my eyes widening as I look at the images on the screen. There are photos of him in royal regalia— looking *ever* so handsome—standing beside people who must be his family, all dressed in finery that screams wealth and power.

I flick through more photos, my heart pounding. Could he be telling the truth? Could this man—this rugged, gorgeous, soup-slinging guy—really be a prince?

I hand the phone back to him. "Okay, but why *here*? People come up to Frozen Heights for all sorts of reasons, and most of them are *not* good."

He tucks his phone away. "You're smart to be cautious. But I swear, I'm here for the hidden beauty of this place. The silence, the solitude—it's peaceful. And I'm used to the climate. Mostly, I'm here because nobody would ever expect me to be here."

I nod. That's true enough.

He slides his large hand over mine. It's a struggle not to gasp at the sudden tingles. "I promise you, JJ, I mean you no harm. I just want to keep you safe until the storm passes."

He seems sincere, his blue eyes open and honest. But I've been burned before, believing things that turned out to be lies. I can't afford to make that mistake again.

"Fine," I say, wrapping the blanket tighter around me. "But as soon as the storm clears, I'm out. I've got a life to get back to, and it doesn't involve getting snowed in with a prince."

He nods, casting his eyes down for a moment. "Understood. Until then, how about we make the best of it? I've got some cards. We might as well enjoy the time we have together?"

Maybe hanging out a little more with this mysterious prince won't be so bad.

But I still have to be careful. As sweet as Val might be, he's still a stranger. And I'm still a girl who doesn't believe in fairy tales.

I have to remember: this is just a temporary escape from reality. And no prince, no matter how charming—*or smoking hot*—is going to change that.

Even if my heart and my body are starting to whisper something else entirely.

CHAPTER 4
VALRIC

"You know, you're not very good at bluffing," JJ laughs, arching an eyebrow.

I chuckle, rearranging my cards. She's bundled up in a blanket, sitting on the floor with her back resting against the sofa, holding her own cards close. Her eyes glimmer with the flames from the fire as she assesses her hand, her lips curved in a smirk. Her blend of wit and hidden vulnerability is driving me insane in the best possible way.

"I would think you'd be pleased that I have a hard time lying," I reply.

She smiles again. Whenever she does that, my pants get a little tighter.

"Believe it or not, royal life doesn't involve a lot of cards," I add. "But I'm quite skilled at other games."

She snorts, a sound that's too cute to be derisive. "Oh yeah? Like what? Chess? Polo? Endurance throne-sitting?"

I laugh, realizing I've done more of that since she's been here than I have in a long while. Her snark is refreshing, such a contrast to the polite, deferential conversation I'm used to at palace functions. "Something like that. But I must admit, I'm enjoying this game immensely."

She rolls her eyes but can't hide her smile. "Well, don't get too comfortable, your highness. I'm about to wipe the floor with your royal butt."

She *is* good. Better than I expected, and I find myself having to concentrate to keep up. But even as I focus on the game, I'm distracted by my opponent. The way her lips purse when she's thinking. The way her eyes light up when she wins a hand. The way her fingers fidget with the pink streaks in her dark hair when she's nervous. It's all intoxicating, alluring, and unbelievably sexy. I've never met anyone that I've been so attracted to.

As we play, we chat. She asks about Thornfjord and my life as a prince, and I find myself sharing stories and recalling memories that I haven't thought about in years. I tell her about the grand balls and the endless diplomatic events, about the beauty of the northern lights and riding through the snow on a sleigh. She listens, her expression rapt, and I can see the wheels turning in her head, her skepticism warring with her desire to believe.

"It does sound magical," she admits.

"It can be, yes. But it's also a lot of responsibility—and expectations, and rules, and duties."

She nods. "I guess it must be hard, always having to live up to other people's ideas of who you should be."

I'm struck by her insight. She seems to get it in a way that few people ever do. I feel a connection to this girl that goes beyond physical attraction, beyond the playful banter and the teasing smiles. It's something deeper, and it takes my breath away.

"What about you?" I ask, shuffling before I deal the next

hand. "What do you do when you're not getting lost in blizzards and doubting men who claim to be princes?"

She smiles. "I'm a library assistant at the Deepwood Mountain Library. I love books—the smell of them, the feel of them. The way they can transport you to another world, you know?"

"I've always loved books, too. The library in the Palace is one of my favorite places to be." I grab my phone. "Want to see?"

"Um, *duh?!*" she replies, and I nearly choke on my sputtered laugh.

"Oh—maybe I shouldn't be saying—"

I shake my head. "Please, don't behave any differently around me. I love this."

She bites her lip and smiles. "Okay, hand over the phone, Val."

"Much better." I chuckle, giving her the phone.

She snatches it. "Holy crap! That's my dream library," she says, eyes glued to the screen. "You even have those sliding ladders and everything!"

"You don't have those at your library?" I ask, genuinely captivated by her honest reaction. "How do you reach the books at the top?"

She scoffs. "Our library is really small." She sighs. "We recently got some large donations to fix it up, and it's ten times better now. Still not this grand, of course. This is lovely."

She hands the phone back to me. "I love working there, though. I work mostly with kids, helping them find books they love…stories that speak to them."

I can see the passion in her eyes, the love she has for her job. It's so pure and sweet that it makes her even more beautiful. "That sounds wonderful," I say. "Books were my escape growing up."

She tilts her head to the side. "What's your favorite book?"

I think for a moment, then grin. *"The Adventures of Huckleberry Finn.* I loved the idea of freedom, of breaking away from society and all its rules."

She giggles. "I can see that. The rebel prince, huh?"

I chuckle, nodding. "Maybe. What about you? What's your favorite book?"

She licks her lips, sending a surge of desire straight to my cock. *"Pride and Prejudice,"* she admits with a blush. "I know it's cliché, but I love the way Elizabeth stands up for herself, the way she challenges Mr. Darcy and makes him see the world differently."

I smile, reaching out to brush one of her pink strands out of her eyes. "It's not cliché at all. It's romantic. And I can see why you love that book. You're a lot like Elizabeth, you know. Strong…independent…not afraid to speak your mind."

She blushes again, looking down at her cards. "Thanks," she murmurs. "So, if you weren't busy being a prince full time, what would you do?"

I lean back, considering her question. "I think I'd like to teach," I eventually say, surprising myself with the admission. "I love kids—their energy, their curiosity. The way they use their imagination can be incredibly inspiring. And I'd love to help them discover the world and see that light in their eyes when they learn something new."

She studies me, nodding, making my heart turn cartwheels. "I can see you doing that. From what I've seen so far, I think you'd be great with kids…and a fun teacher."

I feel a rush of pleasure at her words, a sense of validation that I didn't even know I was seeking.

"Speaking of which…" she continues. "What do you do for fun? Beside rescuing damsels in distress, of course."

I groan. "There's not much rescuing, actually. Most of the time, royal life is painfully dull. There's a lot of networking, making appearances at ribbon cuttings or whatever." I look off into the fire. "*So* many ribbon cuttings…" I turn back to her. "When I'm not dodging my royal duties, I enjoy whittling, though."

She raises an eyebrow. "Whittling? As in carving little soldiers and stuff out of wood?"

"Exactly." I shrug. "It's therapeutic. Grounding. It reminds me of the simpler things in life. Things that matter."

"That's…surprisingly normal. But not exactly what I would expect from a prince."

I smirk. "Well, underneath all the prince stuff, I am just a man, JJ."

She's searching my eyes again. For what, I'm not sure. Then she leans closer.

"Come on, Val. Tell me the *real* reason you wanted to get away and hide."

I sigh, running a hand through my hair. I guess I can tell her. To be honest, I want to share *all* my secrets with JJ. I trust her and I feel like she would understand. "My parents have been pressuring me to marry. I'm thirty-five and time is ticking, in their opinion. But I couldn't care less about marrying to form a political alliance, which is what they want. I'd prefer to marry for love."

Her eyes twinkle. "And you thought you'd find love in the middle of Buttfuck Nowhere, Montana?"

I chuckle. "No. But I did think I'd find peace. A chance to breathe. To figure out what I really want."

She nods, her expression thoughtful. "And have you? Figured out what you want, I mean."

I look at this fiery, beautiful woman who's turned my world upside down in a matter of hours. "I think I'm starting to," I say, my voice low.

She blinks, then looks away, her cheeks flushing slightly. "Well… Good luck, I guess," she whispers.

I can't help it: my gaze goes straight to her mouth and I reach out to cup her cheek, my thumb brushing over her soft lips. Her hazel eyes go wide, and I freeze, worried I may have overstepped a boundary, caught up in the intensity of the moment.

Then she leans in, pressing her lips to mine in a soft, tentative kiss.

God…that's heavenly.

I'm stunned, but only momentarily. Then I clutch her face and kiss her back, pulling her closer, wanting more of her sweetness.

She's suddenly in my lap, her arms wrapping around my neck, deepening the kiss. It's hot, intense, a frenzy of passion and need. I run my hands through her hair, down her back, feeling her curves. She moans, her body melting into mine, and I'm lost, completely and utterly spellbound by her.

Her taste is intoxicating. I can't get enough as I explore her mouth, my tongue dancing with hers. She's so responsive, so alive, and every touch, every desperate sound, drives me wild. I want her, all of her, more than I've ever wanted anything or anyone in my life.

The sharp ping of her phone cuts through the haze of desire, and she pulls back, her eyes wild and her breath coming in ragged gasps. She looks at me, shocked and confused, and then she's scrambling for her phone.

I just sit there, my body aching and my heart pounding. That was more intense than anything I've ever experienced.

An unbidden shudder wracks my body because I know, without a shadow of a doubt, that I'm falling for this woman— falling hard and fast.

And there's nothing I can do to stop it.

CHAPTER 5
JJ

I can't believe it. I just kissed Val.

My first kiss.

That led to...oh my god...*straddling* him, and a make-out session that left me breathless.

Holy shit.

Is this how it's supposed to feel? I don't have any frame of reference, besides what I've read. But my toes curled and my brain short-circuited. I mean, that's gotta mean something.

I touch my lips. They're still tingling. I glance up at Val, and there's a hunger in his eyes, intense and unyielding, that makes my stomach flip-flop. I quickly look away, my heart pounding in my chest.

What the hell am I doing? This is insane. *I'm* insane. This whole SITUATION is insane.

I take a deep breath, trying to collect myself. I need to get a grip and put some distance between us, to remind myself that this is probably all just a crazy, storm-induced fantasy. He can't *possibly* be a prince, despite what he's shown me. Princes just don't come to tiny mountain towns, rescue half-frozen women in blizzards, and kiss like...like...*that*.

But even as I try to convince myself, I can't shake the feeling that there's something about Val that's genuine and sincere and...real. And the scary thing is, I'm starting to believe him. I'm starting to see him as more than just a delusional stranger.

I feel an undeniable pull toward him that goes beyond anything I've ever felt before.

Val clears his throat and runs a hand through his hair. "I'm sorry if I came on too strong there, JJ. I just—"

My phone pings yet *again*.

I grab it off the coffee table and glance at the screen.

"It's Penny," I say. "She's blowing up my phone. My message must've finally gone through."

> what's going on?
>
> are you okay???
>
> rescued by a yeti? Girl, WTAF!!!!

I type out a quick response, assuring her that I'm fine, and that I'm safe, but that I'm stuck in a cabin with a man who claims to be a prince. She instantly texts back wanting details about this mysterious man, and I chuckle as I tell her about Val, making sure to mention how hot he is.

"You're smiling," Val says, and I look up, my cheeks heating. There's a playful smirk on his lips. "What are you saying about me?" He leans over to try and read the screen.

I pull the phone away. "None of your beeswax, mister." Then I stick out my tongue at him.

He laughs, a wicked glint in his eyes. "Oh, really? You think you can keep secrets from me?"

I raise a challenging eyebrow. "I think I can do whatever I want, Your Highness."

He grins, a slow, devilish smile that sends a shiver down my spine. "All right. But I'm warning you… I do love a good chase."

In an instant he's on his feet, lunging toward me. I let cut a shriek, scrambling to dart around the couch. He races after me, laughing. I'm laughing too. It's absurd and childish and completely ridiculous, and it's the most fun I've had in a long time.

He finally catches me, his big arms wrapping around my waist, and he pulls me down onto the couch, pinning me beneath him. I squirm and wriggle, trying to break free, but he's too strong, too solid. He grabs my phone triumphantly, holding it up and out of my reach, grinning.

"Give it back," I demand breathlessly as I make another futile swipe for my phone. Val holds it just out of reach, a smug smile on his face.

"Uh-uh," he teases. "Not until you tell me what you're saying about me."

"No way!" I giggle, reaching up again, but he holds the phone higher. As he does so his shirt rides up, revealing a tantalizing swath of muscled abs and taut skin.

Damn…he's gorgeous. Absolutely gorgeous…

I try to scowl, but the adorable sight of his rumpled clothes and disheveled hair make it impossible. "You leave me no choice."

His brow lifts. "Choice?"

I reach up and slide my fingers over his sides, finding the exact spot that makes him jerk away with a laugh. "Than to do…*this*!" I say, grinning wickedly as I tickle him mercilessly.

Val lets out a yelp, trying to get away, but I'm relentless. My fingers dance over his sides and stomach as he twists and squirms under my touch, laughing breathlessly as he attempts to escape. "Okay, okay!" he finally gasps out between laughs. "You win!"

His body is hot and hard under my hands, and his laughter vibrating through him and into me sets my own body alight.

He manages to capture one of my wrists, pulling it away from his side, but I just switch tactics, using my other hand to tease the sensitive skin just above his waistband. He buckles, laughter bubbling up from deep within him, and I can't help but revel in the power I have over him at this moment.

"JJ," he begs. "Please…"

I slow my torment but don't stop completely, my fingers trailing lightly over his stomach, tracing the lines of his muscles. His skin is smooth and warm, and I can feel the rapid rise and fall of his breathing under my fingertips.

"Please what?" I ask, my voice low and teasing.

He looks down at me, his eyes growing dark. His hand reaches up to stroke my cheek. "Just…please."

I shudder at the raw need in his voice. I lean into his hand, my own stilling on his stomach, feeling the heat, the slight tremble of his muscles.

He hands me my phone. "This can't get out, you know. It would be political suicide if anyone found out the Prince of Thornfjord was ticklish."

I laugh as I take the phone from him. "You have my word."

My gaze locks with his. I can see the hunger there that matches my own. I want him, more than I've ever wanted anyone.

I swallow hard and show him the last message I sent Penny.

> He's smoking hot. Funny, and smart, and kind to a fault. I really like him… Is that crazy?

His smile widens. "I like you too, JJ," he says softly. "A lot. How could I not? You're beautiful, sexy, witty…"

Before I can react, he's pulling me down to him and capturing my lips in a fierce, passionate kiss that sets my body on fire. I'm aching with need, his hard arousal pressing against my hip.

He pulls back momentarily, and we catch our breaths. "Are you sure about this?" he asks, voice gentle. "I don't want to rush you. I don't—"

I cut him off with another kiss, my lips hungry for him. "I'm sure," I whisper into his mouth. "I want this, Val. I want *you*."

Dammit, I'm falling for this man. So hard.

CHAPTER 6
VALRIC

I look down at JJ, her hazel eyes wide and hopeful, her body trembling slightly beneath mine. She's stunning, and I can't believe that she's here with me. That she wants me as much as I want her. I've never felt such an intense, all-consuming need for someone.

"All right," I say. "But we go at your pace, all right?"

She smiles. It hits me straight in the chest. "Okay, but just so you know, I'm not exactly...experienced. I mean, I've never—"

"You're a virgin?"

She nods, her cheeks turning pink.

"Hey." I lift her chin, smiling into her eyes. "That's... wonderful. Special." I pause for a moment. "I should probably tell you—"

"You really *are* a yeti, aren't you?!" she finishes for me, grinning.

I chuckle, shaking my head. "I...um...I've never done this before, either," I finally admit.

The teasing glint in her eye fades. "No. You *cannot* be a virgin, too."

I nod, a wry smile on my lips. "I know it might seem unlikely given my age and my…uh…*status*, for want of a better word. But most of my life has been strictly guarded and controlled when it comes to my love life. Dating as a royal is just…weird. And I never wanted to sleep with someone just for the sake of it. I wanted to find the right person, the right connection." I look into her eyes, heart hammering. "I've finally found that with you, JJ."

I brush my lips against hers, a soft, gentle kiss that deepens as she leans into me. Her hands tentatively explore my chest, her touch setting my skin ablaze. I trail kisses down her neck as my fingers trace the edge of her shirt. "Is this okay?" I murmur.

She nods, holding my gaze as she lifts her arms, allowing me to pull her top over her head and off. Her bare breasts are perfect, fitting neatly into my palms as I cup them, my thumbs circling her nipples. She lets out a moan, her head falling back as I lean down to take one taut peak into my mouth.

"Ohhh," she gasps, her fingers threading through my hair.

I lavish attention on her breasts, quickly learning what kind of touch makes her squirm and where to kiss to make her gasp. Every reaction is a quiet victory, every moan a sweet reward. I start to explore every inch of her, unraveling her piece by heavenly piece.

My hands move to the waistband of her sweatpants. She lifts her hips, helping me slide them down her legs. Her panties follow, leaving her bare before me. I take a moment to appreciate the sight, the firelight casting flickering shadows over her delicious curves.

"You're ravishing, JJ," I say, my voice catching in my throat.

She blushes, her legs instinctively squeezing together. I gently stop her, my hands running up her thighs. "No. Don't hide that beautiful pussy from me…" I plead.

I kneel between her legs, my pulse pounding in my ears. I might not have ever done this before, but I've read enough, fantasized enough…maybe even watched a movie or two…to have an idea. I press my lips to her inner thigh, feeling her muscles tense beneath my mouth. I move higher, my breath hot on her sensitive skin. She squirms, wriggling her hips as I trail kisses over her pussy.

"Val," she breathes. "That feels so good."

I look up, meeting her gaze. "I really don't know what I'm doing, but if you keep telling me what feels good and what doesn't, we'll figure it out together. Sounds like a plan?"

She nods and I dive in, my tongue exploring her folds. She tastes so sweet, like musky nectar, and I'm going mad for it. I find her clit, circling it gently with my tongue.

She lets out a soft cry, her hips bucking against my mouth. "Oh, Val—yes!"

I shudder at her pleasure, gripping her thighs, holding her in place, continuing my exploration.

Her gasps and moans guide me as I slip my tongue further into her wet opening, and her tight heat draws me in.

"God…" she whispers as I find every secret spot, her body gifting me with tiny tremors that make my cock get even harder.

When I begin licking and sucking on her swollen clit, her breaths come even faster, and her body tenses as I bring her closer to the edge. I look up, wanting to see her face as she comes undone. With her eyes closed, lips slightly parted and cheeks flushed, she's breathtaking.

"Val," she gasps, her fingers clenching in my hair. "I'm… I'm… Don't stop. Don't ever stop."

I smile against her skin. "I won't, sweetheart. Come for me," I murmur. "Let go, JJ."

She cries out, her body convulsing and her back arching. I continue to lick and suck, riding out her orgasm with her. I swear, if anything touched my cock right now, I'd explode.

When she finally comes down, her body going limp, I press one last kiss to her sensitive center.

I kiss my way back up her sweat-slicked body, over her stomach, her breasts, her neck, until I'm looking into her eyes...those beautiful, sated, shining eyes. She smiles at me softly in a way that makes my heart ache, makes me want to hold her, protect her, and make her mine...*forever.*

"That was..." She trails off, shaking her head as if at a loss for words.

I grin, kissing her gently, letting her taste herself on my lips. "Just a taste of what's to come," I promise, my voice a low rumble.

She shivers, her eyes darkening. "I want you inside me, Val. I want you to make me truly yours," she whispers. "Please."

I groan, my body responding to her desperate words. I'm so hard it hurts. But I also want to take my time and savor this, making it everything she's ever dreamed it would be.

"Are you sure you're ready for this? Ready for me?"

She nods, her lovely eyes filled with conviction. "Yes, I'm ready."

I smile, my heart pounding in my chest, my body aching with need. As I position myself at her entrance and push into her snug, wet channel I know this is exactly where I'm meant to be.

"How is it, JJ?" I ask, holding back from thrusting into her delicious heat.

"It's...a little tight," she says, her voice wavering.

"I'll stop."

"No—don't." She wraps her legs around me, biting her lip. "Just go slow…and kiss me."

I grin. "Gladly, sweetheart." I kiss her sweet mouth and begin to rock my hips forward. The pleasure is *blinding*. "*Jeesuuus*… You feel incredible, JJ," I say through clenched teeth.

She chuckles and I feel her body relax, her arms tightening around me. "Yes, it's getting so much better."

I pump a little harder and she gasps. "Oh, god… Yeah, keep going. More of *that*."

I drive into her again and again, making her moan like crazy.

I'm lost in her, surrendering to the sheer, overwhelming intensity of it all. Still, way back in my mind, there's a niggling fear. Of allowing someone else to control my heart so completely.

But as I near my climax, I make a solemn promise to myself not to let that fear win. I won't have this brilliant, amazing woman slip through my fingers. We'll find a way forward.

She's the first person who's made me feel seen, loved me for the man I am, not the prince. She's made me feel like me.

I thrust deeper into her, changing the angle.

She arches up. "I'm going to—" she pants.

"Do it, my love," I growl, right in her ear.

Suddenly her pussy is squeezing my cock in delicious waves, her orgasm slamming through her.

She cries out, and god, I'm going to be right behind her.

I pump into her hard and fast, then suddenly realize we never talked about protection. Right before I tumble over that edge, I pull out and stroke my cock, sending hot, white seed splattering over her belly and breasts.

The sight nearly makes me pass out and I roar, my climax wracking my body.

"Wow. I never imagined it could be like that," she whispers, as we lie on the couch recovering.

"Me either," I admit, my heart still pounding.

CHAPTER 7
JJ

V al and I moved into his bedroom to cuddle under his thick down comforter after a couple more rounds of lovemaking, and I wake up to the early morning light peeking into the window.

My body is deliciously sore in places I didn't know could hurt, and I can feel myself smiling like a goofball. Val's chiseled arm is draped protectively over me as memories of the night before flood my mind—of Val, his touch, his body, his words...it was all intense and so, so beautiful.

It was everything I never knew I wanted.

But as the haze of sleep and satisfaction lifts, reality comes crashing down. He's still sleeping peacefully, his handsome face relaxed, hair tousled... But in the cold light of day, I can't help but feel a wave of doubt wash over me.

This is too good to be true, too perfect, too...unreal. He's a prince, for crying out loud.

A prince.

With royal duties and obligations and responsibilities that do not include someone like me.

I slowly slide out from his embrace, being careful not to

wake him. I gather my clothes, my mind spinning. I need to leave. Need to put some distance between us before I get in too deep and start believing in this impossible fantasy.

Even as I pull on my pants, sweater, and boots, I can't ignore the voice in the back of my mind telling me to stay and to fight. *To believe.* The voice that's telling me that this is worth taking a chance on.

I shake my head, pushing the hope and the longing and the desire aside. No. It's ridiculous to think this would work. Absurd. It's—

"Where are you going, JJ?"

I jump as Val's voice, still husky with sleep, cuts through my thoughts. I turn, my heart pounding in my chest, to see him propped up on one elbow, his eyes locked on me.

I swallow, trying to find the right words to rationalize everything. "I...I was just...I mean, I thought it would be better if I..." I trail off, gesturing vaguely to the door, to the world outside, to the reality that's waiting to tear us apart.

Val sits up, the bedding slipping down to his waist. His chest is bare, his muscles taut, and it's a real struggle to keep my eyes on his face and my thoughts on track.

"Better if you what, JJ?" he asks softly. "Snuck out before we could talk and figure this out? Before we could decide *together* what this means and where it goes?"

I take a deep breath. "Val, come on," I plead. "You know this can't work. Can't last. You're a prince, and I'm...just me. I'm a nobody."

Val's expression darkens, his eyes flashing. "You're *not* a nobody, JJ," he says firmly. "You're not 'just' anything. You're wonderfully, unapologetically you. And that's more than enough for me. That's *everything.*"

I shake my head. "That's very sweet, Val. But it's not reality. Think about it: you have royal obligations. You need to marry a princess or at least a person with a title, not someone like me."

Val swings his legs over the side of the bed and quickly strides over to me. He takes my hands in his, his grip firm and warm. "*Fuck* titles—pardon my language. And fuck duties or obligations or responsibilities. I don't care about those, not when it comes to us. I care about you and how you make me feel, about how we make each other feel. I care about our connection and our *love*."

My heart stutters. *Love*. He's in love with me.

"I know it's fast," he continues, "but I know it's right, JJ. I feel it right here." He points to his heart.

I look up at him, my emotions tumbling over each other. "I love you, too, Val. And I want to give in to this. To *us*. But I'm so scared. I'm scared that this is too good to be true, too perfect to be real, too much to last."

Val smiles softly and tenderly. It melts my heart. "It *is* perfect, it *is* real, and it's definitely worth fighting for."

I take a deep breath and decide to take a leap of faith and just let myself *believe*. "Okay," I say, my voice steady. "Let's fight for our love."

He grins, his blue eyes lighting up as he pulls me into his arms, his lips finding mine in a searing, passionate kiss. And somehow, there in his arms, all my fears and doubts fade away, and all that remains is love.

Pure, fierce, all-consuming love.

When we finally pull apart, we're both breathless and grinning like fools. "So... What's the plan?" I ask excitedly.

He laughs, a low, sexy sound that sends heat shooting between my legs. "First, I think we need to get you introduced to my parents. I'll explain the situation, make them understand that I've found my princess—even if she's not exactly who they were expecting."

I groan, burying my face in his chest. "Oh god, what if they hate me? What if they think I'm not good enough for you?"

He tilts my chin up, forcing me to look at him. "They won't hate you, JJ. They'll love you, just like I do."

I smile, my heart swelling with love and hope.

"I'm not letting you go for anything or anyone, JJ. You're stuck with me now," he laughs. "For better or for worse, in sickness and in health, till death do us part."

I beam at him. "Well, when you put it that way, how can I resist...Your Highness?"

He leans in and kisses me again.

My heart is filled with happiness. Together, with love on our side, we can conquer anything.

EPILOGUE - VALRIC

SIX MONTHS LATER

As I carefully steer the SUV up the winding roads of Deepwood Mountain, I steal glances at JJ. Six months ago, I never would have imagined a life engaged to a woman who challenges and completes me, and who's given me the courage to stand up to my royal family and carve my own path. And yet, here we are.

We decided to split our time between Thornfjord and Deepwood Mountain. We haven't quite ironed out all the details yet, but we're confident we can make it work.

JJ's been quiet since we got on the plane in Thornfjord to come back here. Her fingers absentmindedly twirl the pink streaks in her hair. I know she's overwhelmed, drawn into the whirlwind that is royal life, despite the outpouring of love from my family who understand what I see in her.

I reach over, squeezing her hand. "Penny for your thoughts, Princess JJ?"

She scoffs lightly, grinning. "Please, Val. I'm not a princess yet."

I grin. "Soon, though. You might as well get used to it."

She rolls her eyes, but her smile widens. "What have you done to me, my prince? *I'm* supposed to be the cynic in this partnership, not the one getting caught up in the magic of it all."

"Ah, but that's the beauty of teamwork, isn't it?" I turn onto the familiar road leading to the Deepwood Mountain Inn. "You make me want to be a better prince, and I make you believe in happy endings."

She leans over and kisses my cheek. "Good point. But don't think I'll stop reading romance novels any time soon, just because I'm living one."

I laugh. "I wouldn't have it any other way, my sweet."

We pull up to the Inn and I park, my heart pounding with excitement. I've been planning this surprise for weeks, coordinating with JJ's family, friends, and co-workers. I can't wait to see her face when it all goes down.

I help her out of the SUV, and her brow furrows when she sees the unusually crowded parking lot. "What's with all the cars?" she asks suspiciously.

I shrug innocently, trying to keep my facial expression neutral. "Who knows. Maybe everyone wanted to welcome the future Princess of Thornfjord."

She smirks. "Yeah, or maybe you're *up to something.*"

We walk up to the front entrance and the door of the Inn bursts open, a chorus of cheers erupting. JJ's eyes go wide as she takes in the crowd all shouting "Surprise!"

She turns to me, her mouth agape. "What is all this?"

I grin, wrapping an arm around her waist. "I figured since you've been so gracious in embracing my world, it's only fair I embrace yours. Welcome to your engagement party, princess."

We're swept into the Inn and instantly enveloped by the warmth and love of friends and family. JJ's mother pulls her into a tight hug, tears streaming down her face. "I'm so happy for you, sweetheart," she says, looking at me over JJ's shoulder. "And you, Valric, thank you for bringing our girl such happiness."

I bow slightly. "It's I who should be thanking you for raising such an incredible daughter."

The party is in full swing, laughter and music filling the air. I watch JJ drift from group to group, her face glowing, and can't help but feel a swell of pride and love. This is the life I want—not stuffy royal parties and political maneuvering, but this.

Real people, real laughter.

Real love.

I make my way to the bar and order a drink, then feel a hand clap me on the back. I turn to see JJ's father, his eyes shining with emotion. "You did good, Val," he says, handing me a small, worn book. "I think it's time I gave you this."

I look down and realize with a start it's a collection of Nordic fairy tales, much like one I have back in Thornfjord. I flip through the pages, seeing notes and illustrations scattered throughout. "This is—"

"JJ's," he smiles. "She asked me to give it to you. She's had it since she was a little girl. Always dreamed of her own fairy tale. And you know, I think she's found it in you."

I smile warmly, touched that he would entrust me with something so precious. Then I tuck the book into my pocket.

As the night goes on I get drawn into various conversations, sharing stories. JJ and I talk with Mitch and Penny, and my cheeks hurt from laughing so hard. But finally, I pull JJ into a quiet corner, wanting to get her alone.

She smiles at me, her eyes reflecting the soft glow of the twinkly lights strung from the ceiling. "Having fun, Your Highness?" she winks.

I wrap my arms around her, pulling her close. "Yes, but even more now," I say, leaning down to kiss her. As our lips meet, a light snow begins to fall outside, reminding me of the night we met.

Our sweeping tale may have started in a blizzard, but it's grown into something so warm. And as I hold JJ in my arms, I know that this is just the beginning of our adventure together —the Nordic prince and his enchanting princess, a love story written in the snow-covered peaks of Frozen Heights.

Now that we've come to the end of the Frozen Heights series...what's next?

McCafferty Mechanics
Featuring the red-hot motorcycle mechanics of McCafferty Customs in Deepwood Mountain

Whether it's romantic midnight rides under the stars, steamy kisses against chrome and steel, or searing touches amidst the grease and gears, these irresistible men are ready to rev your engines and take you on the ride of a lifetime.

Check out the McCafferty Mechanics series page here:
https://www.lexihayes.com/series/mccafferty-mechanics/

You can sign up for my newsletter via my website:
www.lexihayes.com
It's the best way to hear about new and upcoming releases, plus get access to subscriber exclusives and bonus content.

And as always, if you liked this story, please post a review on any of your preferred platforms. Reviews are the lifeblood of independent authors like me, and I welcome your opinions and feedback.

Thanks for reading!

ABOUT THE AUTHOR

Lexi writes short, steamy, over-the-top romance with a heaping dose of humor. She is a long-time superhero lover, book sniffer, and Mr. Darcy fanatic. Raised in the same SoCal city as Will Ferrell, she now resides in sweltering Las Vegas with her husband and two spoiled cats. She dreams of lush green foliage, ocean waves, and Henry Cavill. Or Tom Hiddleston. It's a toss-up really. ;)

Join Lexi's mailing list for new and upcoming releases (and exclusive content!) here: www.lexihayes.com